MEMOIRS OF A HITMAN

Johnny Mack has spent most of his life as a South London gangster. For two decades Johnny threw himself wholeheartedly into a life of crime. From jump ups, tie ups, bank robbery, unlicensed boxing and eventually drug distribution on a big scale upon London's notorious housing estates. He ran illegal drinking clubs – known as 'Spielers', everything was grist to Johnny's mill. Drug addiction finally brought Johnny crashing down to earth. But he came back from the brink of self destruction and has risen again to become the man he is today.

Johnny has now turned his life away from crime and has become the successful author of two autobiographies and one novel. Johnny is optimistic that his autobiographies will soon be made into a feature film or a TV drama serialisation chronicling the life and crimes of this true underworld villain and all round chap.

Not only has Johnny turned his back on a life of crime and addictions, he is now a counsellor helping others who are on the wrong path, the very path Johnny had once walked for many years. Johnny uses his life experiences to help the young and old, whether it is a kid hooked on heroin and doing crime or a middle-aged family man with a drink problem. This is all within Johnny's grist and he is genuine with giving his help and experience to others.

Published Work:

Dunpeckham (2008)
Olympia Publishers
ISBN: 9781905513505

Landed on the Moon (2011)
Olympia Publishers
ISBN: 9781848971530

MEMOIRS OF A HITMAN

Johnny Mack

MEMOIRS OF A HITMAN

Olympia Publishers
London

www.olympiapublishers.com
OLYMPIA PAPERBACK EDITION

A CIP catalogue record for this title is
available from the British Library.

ISBN: 978-1-84897-169-1
This is a work of fiction.
Names, characters, places and incidents originate from the writer's
imagination. Any resemblance to actual persons, living or dead, is purely
coincidental.

First Published in 2012

Olympia Publishers
60 Cannon Street
London
EC4N 6NP

Printed in Great Britain

To Hannah who gave me the inspiration to be able to create the main characters in this novel

&

Tony and Jean

Acknowledgments

I would like to express my sincere gratitude to the Cancer UK trial team at Queen Alexander Hospital, Cosham UK. If it were not for them then this novel would never have been possible. A big thank you is due to Guy Robinson for his help and support whilst producing this novel. Caroline Diamond for her work as senior editor; she has done a magnificent job with the final process of the production of this novel.

Chapter One

My double life

According to the National Meteorological Office, it was the coldest night for that month since records began. It was force ten winds with sleet and snow. My barometer registered minus 4c and even though I was inside my car, ice had developed on the inside of the windows and my breath resembled steam as I exhaled. It was a bitterly cold, pitch-black noisy night and the time was just coming up to four in the morning. I was parked up in a secluded spot in an unlit, tree-lined suburban side road of Victorian two-up-two-down terraced houses. Just sitting, waiting.

I had been to this location quite a few times over the last four weeks at exactly the same time and parked up in the same place. My reason for being there was to watch and learn the routine of a certain unsavoury character called Victor Malevich. Victor had been a Serbian fighter in the Bosnian War and he had moved to the U.K. It seemed he had settled in well and had found regular employment at a local factory. Every morning like clockwork, he would leave his house at four on the dot in his Volkswagen camper van and drive the five miles to his work-place. There he would complete his shift by two in the afternoon; then return home. This he did four days a week and he seemed no different from thousands of other honest, hardworking people. Victor's family consisted of a wife, two young children and two dogs, and from my observations, he was friendly with his neighbours. He would talk to them in a sociable manner after his return from work while taking his dogs for walks. To those around him he acted and presented himself as Mr. Average. I was given this contract six weeks earlier and it was no different from the ten contracts I had carried out previously. With all of them I would go through the same format: find out where they were located and watch their movements to get to know their routines. Once that was established and I was completely satisfied that I could carry out my assignment, I would go to work. My task for that morning was to kill Victor.

This job was a particularly easy one for me. First, I had to trace Victor and to do that, I used my contacts in the Civil Service. These contacts of mine could find a needle in a haystack if asked. Once I had his location, I would then plot up and follow the procedure I had been taught by my peers.

I had never heard of Victor before I was given this contract, so he meant nothing to me. He was just another number and another payday, just like the other ten I had snuffed out before him. To be able to do my job, I had to take control of my emotions and fears, and to do that I had to be able to justify the reason for the contract so that I could walk away with a clear conscience. Sounds cold-hearted to some, but for me it was now a way of life. In my given occupation I had to be extra careful. All the planning had to be right and if just one thing did not go to plan, then I would simply bail. I had to because one mistake could send me to a place where I would spend the next thirty years behind bars and ultimately, at my age of forty-seven, I would die there.

All my contracts came to me via a phone contact and the person on the other end was a complete stranger to me. I knew nothing about her and the only reason I worked for her was because of the fact she was put in touch with me via the Firm I was involved with from my days working in the organised crime fraternity. I had worked and lived as what some would call a 'gangster' for twenty-two of my forty-seven years on this planet. My work varied from extortion to armed robbery, and as my gangster career progressed, so did the work and with that, came respect. As I gained more respect, new avenues opened up for me to earn large amounts of money. Respect, however, could not be bought but had to be earned and I had earned quite a lot over the years.

I stuck to the rules: no grassing, never fuck over one of your own and never question what was asked of me. Quite simple rules really and they were not hard to follow, though I did know a few who broke them and they paid dearly for their mistakes. My peers taught me very well from the beginning and I adapted easily to the ways of organised crime. Over the coming years I worked my way up the promotion structure of respect. It was similar to working for a large consortium, the only difference being we never asked or waited for people to invest in our business. We just went ahead and took it and if they complained about it, then we would give them something worse to complain about. Our investment structure was quite unique.

When I 'retired' I was given my first hit. I had signed the death warrant for nine people in my time as a gangster and handed the contracts out to those that worked for us, but now I was handed one to do myself. The reason was because I had gone to see my boss Fred and explained to him that I wanted out of the business to nurse my sick partner Hannah who had been diagnosed with a tumour on the brain that could go bang at any moment. You would think the reason I was giving was good enough for anyone who had an ounce of compassion, to let me go. My boss Fred was a ruthless villain and a fair man to some, and I had the utmost respect for him. We had always worked well together and not once did he have cause to bollock me or suspect me of any dodgy dealing. He knew I was a trusted and loyal foot soldier who had plenty of respect for him and played the game with a straight deck of cards. I had never known anyone retire from my line of work unless they were six foot under or doing a thirty stretch in *Belmarsh*, so I was in unknown territory when I asked to leave.

'Retire Jack? Why the fuck do you want to fucking retire?'

'Fred, I need to look after Hannah. There's a good chance she won't pull through after those fucking butchers at the hospital have finished cutting that out of her. I need to be there for her and Jack Junior as much as possible'

Fred paused for a moment then said: 'Look Jack, we all love Hannah and we know how much you care for her, but the truth is you can't just walk away from us. You know too much.'

What he had said to me made me feel as if I was not trusted, which hurt my feelings big time, so I squared up to Fred and replied angrily:

'Fred, are you suggesting that I'm a grass? Have I not been a staunch, trustworthy geezer? In all the years I have worked for your family have you or they ever suspected me of any wrongdoing? Come to think of it, have I ever complained when I've been given the shit work that your lot couldn't sort out for yourselves?'

Fred got up from his large leather swivel chair and stood opposite me looking at me intensely with his shark eyes, puffing on a Cuban cigar. In front of him was his large oval shaped, leather topped regency desk and from knowledge gained over the years, I knew that in the right hand drawer was a .45 automatic. I also knew Fred could be a psychotic maniac if crossed. I was walking on thin ice with him but I was determined to stand my ground because my Hannah was my life. She had stuck by me through thick and thin, including all the shit times, and now it was my turn to stick by her. Fred just stood looking at me rolling the cigar in his mouth with his left hand and with the other resting on the desk as if he was deciding what to do with me.

'You think I'm a heartless bastard don't you Jack?'

I replied quietly 'Yes Fred… to those that take fucking liberties with you, but I'm not one of them. My reason is good enough for you to let me go with no comebacks. Hannah needs me more than you do at this moment.'

Fred said 'I don't see why you can't just take a holiday and come back to us when she gets better.'

'Fred, there is a good chance she's not going to get better mate. Her condition is advanced and I need to be with her constantly till the end if need be. The quack told me straight that it was a fifty-fifty if she pulls through, but Han doesn't realise how serious her condition is.

'How long has she got Jack?'

I paused and then said softly: 'Six to twelve months if she's lucky. She's been a brave girl because she put off the operation until Jack Junior was born, but they are saying at the hospital that there's only an even chance with the operation and a bit of luck. '

'I'm sorry to hear that Jack, truly I am. Let's hope she gets a result with the op.'

I said with respect. 'Thanks Fred. I was hoping you would understand because Han and I made a pact when we first got together that if one of us got ill, then the other would look after them till they got better or pegged it.'

Fred still tried to persuade me that leaving would be unwise because it wasn't just down to him. Even though he was the boss, he had members of his family who would not see things the way he did, and that could cause problems for me if I wasn't careful.

I asked Fred if he would have a word with the others on my behalf and let me know the score.

'Will do Jack. I'll get back to you, ok?'

I replied with relief and said: 'Thanks Fred, I'll wait for your answer.'

When I was outside his office, my feelings were a mixture of elation and anxiety. The elation came from the fact that I had just fronted up to one of the most feared gangsters since the Kray twins. The anxiety came from the fact that I would have to wait for an answer. After all, I was dealing with people who could wipe me off the planet in an instant, and if my request for retirement was refused, then I would know fuck all about it until some cunt was standing in front of me with a gun pointed at my head.

That evening I mulled over all the years I had worked for the family, trying to remember if at any time I had given them reason to think I had been a wrong'un. I couldn't think of anything because, as I've already said, I had always been loyal and honest with them. But no amount of thinking could take away that fear and anxiety. I knew I was staunch, but did they? I went on home to be with my Hannah. She was a great girl and I loved her dearly.

We first met shortly after my divorce from my first wife. She was twenty years my junior and was beautiful with the body of a top catwalk model.

After a few weeks of knowing each other we became an item and got engaged three years into our relationship. Our problems started after she became pregnant with Jack Junior. Six months into her pregnancy she was diagnosed with a tumour on the brain and to make matters worse, we were told the operation she needed could result in us losing our baby. Hannah wanted a baby so much that she refused the op until our son was born. I had already had four kids with my ex wife and it seemed strange to me to be starting a family all over again, but the truth was I loved it.

Han never really knew what I did for a living. She guessed it wasn't legal but never asked too many questions. Even when I would come home at all hours she would never say a word. There was one occasion when she really got worried about the type of work I was doing because she found something in my clothes.

I had been instructed to punish a geezer who had been constantly late with his payments. We grabbed him off the street and took him to a lock-up to have a chat. He and his partner had been clients of ours for some time, but they were now getting greedy and decided to start fucking our Firm about with their payments. My job was to teach them a lesson that they would never forget; and that's exactly what I did. After tying the geezer to a chair and gagging him, I cut one forefinger off of each hand and gave him a few slashes of the face with a cut throat razor; just enough to get his attention. Believe me that geezer was promising me the earth by the time I had finished with him. I was to deliver one of his fingers to his partner and the other was to go back to Fred as proof of my work; a bit like a job sheet receipt. Anyway, I delivered the finger to his partner. That quickly got his attention and he managed to come up with the money he owed the Firm. It was difficult for me to hand over the other digit that day because Fred was on a bit of business himself. So I went home with it thinking that I would hide it in the fridge till the next morning. My house at that time was hectic, what with newborn Jack and Hannah going through post-natal depression. I forgot to put the fucking thing in the fridge and kept it in my pocket wrapped in a handkerchief.

During that evening Hannah decided to do some washing because I had a few blood spots on my clothes. She washed everything I had been wearing that day, including the geezer's fucking finger. Half way through the wash the machine decided to breakdown and Hannah went about trying to clear the filter and, you guessed it, she came across the finger. With that she let out a scream that could be heard a mile away. It took me some time to talk my way out of that one but thank fuck she was wise enough not to keep on about it. However, it was the last time she would do any washing for me without me first checking my pockets.

Two days after my meeting with Fred I was called to his office. It was obvious to me that some sort of decision had been made on my request for early retirement. As I entered his office I was a bit apprehensive because he was sitting with Joey, a fucking heartless murdering maniac who was responsible for most of the hits that took place through our Firm. I was thinking to myself 'What the fuck is he doing here?' and it was then that Fred said to me: 'Come in Jack, pull up a chair.'

I said my hellos to Fred and Joey and sat in a big leather chair when Joey says to me: 'You want out then Jack?'

I looked at Fred as if to say to him 'What the fuck has it got to do with this fucking nutter?' when Fred ordered:

'Answer him then Jack.'

So I started to reiterate the reasons I had already given to Fred.

'Yeah Joey I want out mate because Han's not too bright at the moment and…'

Joey cut me short and said: 'I know all about it Jack and I'm sorry to hear about your missus, so there's no need to explain yourself to me.'

I sensed a bit of disrespect and in the way Joey had cut me short and considering I did not respect him that much anyway, I answered in a similar manner.

'Then why ask, Joey?

By his look I knew he sensed the returned contempt in my answer. Like all criminals, he was extra sensitive with an ego the size of a mountain.

Fred looked across at me and said: 'Jack, are you sure you want to quit?'

I knew from Fred's facial expression and the tone of his voice that I was dancing a fine line here. But I was determined to see it through without showing any fear or weakness. This pair of bastards would feed on both given the chance, and I was not prepared to give them a free lunch, so I played the game.

'I'm sure Fred. If Han doesn't make it, then I'm no good to no one mate. I have to put my boy first because he will need me more than ever.'

Joey piped up and said: 'What will you do Jack?'

I answered Joey. 'What do you mean, what will I do?'

'Money Jack, what will you do for money?'

'I've got a few quid put away so I'll probably get a car sales pitch or something like that. To be honest I hadn't thought that far ahead yet.'

Fred came into the conversation. He got up from behind his desk then walked towards me with his brandy and cigar in hand and said: 'There might be a solution that could help your situation Jack.'

I looked up at Fred and said: 'I'm all ears Fred, what's on your mind then?'

Fred said. 'Well Jack, Joey here, is looking for someone to work part-time for a client of his and I think that if you accepted his job offer, that it would not only help you out financially, but still keep you close to us and that means problem solved.'

I could guess what Joey's part-time work would be but asked under the pretence of ignorance.

'What is it then Fred?'

He smirked as he said: 'Well, you know what Joey does for us don't you?'

I now said knowingly: 'I've been about long enough to know what Joey does Fred. I've given him quite a few targets in the past to whack.'

'Well that's nice and clear then: you know what we want from you. It won't be full-time work, just every now and then. And the money's good. What do you think then Jack?'

I had to be really cautious how I replied to this job offer because if I said 'no', then I could expect to get the rough end of the stick and by that, I mean a bullet in the fucking nut. It was obvious that Fred had pulled a few strings and seeing that no one had ever retired before, I was being offered a substitute solution. Therefore, I was expected to react as if I was grateful.

'Thanks Fred I'll do it as long as I'm not at it all the time because, like I said, I've got Hannah and Jack Junior to think about.'

Fred turned to Joey and said 'Well Joey, what do you think?'

Joey just smiled and said: 'Perfect Fred, just perfect.'

I sat there looking at these two fucking lunatics, wondering what the fuck had I just got myself into.

Fred then said casually: 'On your way then Jack. You're now officially retired, so keep those ears of yours open son because you will be getting a call shortly. Keep that phone of yours close. Ok mate?'

I had learnt not to ask too many questions and just nodded and left for home wondering what the fuck I was going to tell Hannah. She had got used to my work routines and now I was to have more time on my hands. I decided to tell her that Fred had given me time off to be with her and Jack Junior until she was over her forthcoming operation at the local butchers' shop. I hated that hospital because I went in there with a bullet wound a few years before. The shell had entered through my left shoulder and exited out through my neck. Lucky for me it never hit any arteries or vital organs. The doctor who operated on me made a fucking mess of my neck and I ended up with an infection that did more damage than the poxy bullet. Not surprisingly my confidence was knocked a bit when I found out that Han was to have her op there.

Hannah was well pleased that I would be around to help her with Jack Junior, even though she never really showed it. She's a determined and somewhat stubborn person who does not give into things, especially pain and illness. She knew that I knew that she was struggling, but she tried her hardest to hide it. After two exhausting but pleasant days with her and the boy, the phone call I had been expecting came. It was short and sweet and the voice on the end told me to go to Victoria Station and pick up a parcel from lost property using a moody name. Once I collected the parcel, I opened it up in my car. Inside were two guns: one a berretta and the other a 45 automatic; both with silencers. There was also an untraceable mobile phone and a large envelope with the details of my new dodgy bank account in the Seychelles. Lastly, there was the info on the hit, including times, places and his photograph. I studied the photo, but never recognised the face.

The people I was now employed by didn't hang about; this hit had to be done that afternoon because the target would be at the perfect place: a particular golf course with which I was familiar. The info on my target was that he would be playing his round of golf alone because he was getting himself familiar with the course for a forthcoming tournament. It was pointed out that this afternoon would be exceptionally quiet on the course and the sixteenth green would be the perfect place to carry out the job. From my own knowledge of the course, the sixteenth green was out of sight of all the other holes because it was positioned in a hollow, almost like a basin area. The bonus for me was that it was edged by a wooded area with plenty of cover so it would be simple for me to tuck myself up and wait for my victim to pop his head up.

At two o'clock that afternoon I was plotted up in the wooded area by sixteenth green. My target had already teed-off his round of golf alone an hour and a half before. I observed him from the car park just before positioning myself on the green. It was now just a waiting game and my calculations, based on his golf handicap, suggested to me that this geezer would be sticking his ugly mug into view within the next ten minutes.

The information pack was accurate about the quietness of the course because there were only three pairs of golfers playing at that time and there were about ten minute intervals between each pair's tee-off. I learned later that day as to why the course was so quiet. Not being a football fan, I had no idea that there were play-offs live on TV that very afternoon. This showed me how much thought and planning had gone into organising this hit and I felt relieved that I was working for professionals; real clever people.

I was dressed in overalls because it would lessen the chance of forensics. It was 1995 and forensic scientists were making many major breakthroughs, which was now making it harder for criminals to get off the hook. On all work like this you would have to destroy all your clothes afterwards, usually by fire. It was also much cheaper to destroy a pair of overalls than a three piece suit.

I heard a voice in the distance shout 'FORE!' And just then a golf ball clattered into a tree and landed just on the edge of the long grass within four metres of where I was tucked up in the wooded area near the edge of the green. I would've liked to have taken my hat off to the geezer. Not only was it a blinding shot for me to get in position, it was also a hole which was completely out of sight of the player. Now I knew why he was getting familiar with the course.

Five minutes later I heard the sound of the wheels of a golf trolley with its clubs clanging about in the bag. Then my man came into sight. First he stood on the crest of the basin wearing his three-quarter length plus fours and bright yellow jumper. He was looking intently for his ball as I was crouched just behind a tree with shrubbery either side, completely motionless. Then the sound of the trolley started again and as I looked up, he was heading straight for me. My nerves were being tested because I had a slight tremor in both legs and arms along with a cold sweat running down my back. When he got to the ball's location he was actually within spitting distance of me. I could even hear the fucker breathing and muttering to himself. I watched him as he turned towards my position to pull a putter from his golf bag. He then turned his back on me to position himself. I slowly stood upright without making a sound, levelled and aimed the berretta complete with silencer at his head and fired once. There was the dull thud of the gun firing, then instantaneously the splatter of blood, bone and hair as the bullet entered the back of his head, followed by a heavy thump as his body hit the deck face down. I stepped out of the brush and took four steps towards him. I was now standing right over his twitching body and fired two more shots to the head thinking to myself: *job done.*

I took a thorough look around the surrounding area and was confident enough to know that there was no one about. Then, acting speedily, I put the gun away and bent down and grabbed his ankles to drag him into the undergrowth. I struggled a bit because this geezer was a big man. Once he was hidden out of sight, I went back and grabbed his golf trolley and hid that next to his body. I went to where I had put the last two shells into him and retrieved the casings and then had a quick look to see if anything else was lying about. I noticed some small bone fragments in a pool of blood in the long grass, so I just covered it with some shrubbery. By covering my tracks and hiding the body I was giving myself time to get away calmly and unrushed with the knowledge that it would take some time for him to be found. By then I would be well and truly gone and out of the way.

That was my introduction to the 'hit man business'. He was not the first geezer I had snuffed out though. Ten years prior, I had killed a geezer with my bare hands because he and two of his cronies thought I was an easy mugging victim. Little did they know that I had been beating and torturing people for a good many years. I felt no remorse or pity for that piece of shit because I fucking hated muggers. To me they were scum, especially if they mugged old ladies or helpless drunks. Anyway, that's how I justified it and I have never lost a night's sleep over it either. But this type of work was to be very different because I would know nothing at all about my target and so feel no anger towards him. I had to train my thoughts and emotions; think of it as strictly business. It was obvious to me that he had pissed someone off badly enough for them to pay fifty grand or more to have him whacked. I acknowledged that he was a wrong'un and had fucked up. The punishment he received might be by some people's standards very harsh, but the fact was it was obligatory to the code of conduct of the business he was in. Quite simple thinking really and that's how I became able to deal with it and sleep tight at night.

*

Hannah went in for her operation and right up to her going into theatre, she kept up her bravado and attitude of 'I'll be alright Jack.' I had never met anyone like her before. She had more guts than some of the toughened villains I had known. The night before she went into hospital I had entered the house very quietly, not wanting to wake Jack Junior. I crept up the stairs and as I reached the top landing, I noticed that our bedroom door was half open. As I entered the room I noticed Han was at the side of our bed kneeling with her hands clasped together. She was startled at first and then briefly annoyed. Finally, she started jokingly threatening me with all sorts of sadistic torture if I ever told anyone of what I had just seen. I had total admiration for her because it showed me that this tough, knowledgeable, streetwise woman was really underneath scared and frightened of what was happening to her. Praying, she told me, was helping her get through this difficult time and if I had the notion she had gone all 'God like', then I had better think again. Bless her for that because she was one strong-willed and proud person and disapproved of weakness.

The most worrying time of my life came just after the op. We were told that the tumour had been completely removed, but there was a possibility of a future brain haemorrhage because the bleeding had weakened certain arteries by putting more pressure on them. Now it would be a waiting game to see if another bleed would appear. I was determined to get her body strong with the kind of protein food that weightlifters and athletes use to get the best performance out of their bodies. Her immune system had to be strong which meant Han couldn't afford to catch so much as a cold. One cough or sneeze could, in fact, kill her.

It was a fucking hard time for me over the first few months of her recovery. I had never been through anything like this before and I found myself doing everything from changing nappies to shopping at *Tesco's*. But it was worth it just to see my Han get well. It would take about a year and a half for her hair to grow back to a decent length so she could have it styled the way she liked it. Before the operation she had beautiful long straight black hair down to her waist. Just prior to the op she decided to shave the lot off so it would grow back evenly. At first she wouldn't leave the house except for hospital trips because of what she thought other people might think of her. I tried to help her and started being a real house husband, taking care of everything else; even taking Jack Junior out to the local mother and baby club three times a week!

During that difficult period I was asked to work a few times and all the contracts went off without a hitch: 'nice and sweet, job done' as I would say. I was content to deal with the people I was working for because their professionalism was outstanding and their payments were always on time.

Han had continued to get well and as time went by, she became her usual self. That gorgeous smile of hers returned and she started living life to the full again. She knew that she had to make the most of each day because, as she would often remind me, that day could be her last – an ironic statement to someone who was in the business of ending people's lives. But she knew fuck all of the work I was doing and, as I've already said, she never asked too many questions.

*

It was one minute to four in the morning and there I was, in the rear of Victor's Volkswagen Camper crouched just behind the drivers' seat. All the windows were iced up and I was now just waiting for Victor to get in.

Victor was very quiet when leaving his house in the morning. I had been watching his movements and he had a routine. This consisted of getting into his camper and without starting the engine, he would roll the van backwards from his drive which was on a slight incline into the road, also on a hill, and then coast silently downhill for twenty or thirty yards before bump starting the van. I suspected he did not want to wake everyone up in the neighbouring houses, especially at that time in the morning, because a Volkswagen engine can make a racket when started. I did wonder what our Vic had done to deserve a visit from me because, from my observations, he seemed a normal, considerate geezer, not like the others I had whacked who had all seemed a bit dodgy. I trained myself to treat it as strictly business and quickly put those thoughts to the back of my mind and concentrated on the job in hand.

I heard Victor's front door quietly close and his footsteps crunching down on fresh snow as he made his way to the van. I pulled out a large screwdriver from my overalls. I had purposely grinded the head into a point which converted it into a fourteen inch chiv. This weaponry was common in jails all over the world because it was effective, quick and deadly if put into the right place.

Victor was now clearing the ice and snow from his windscreen and when that was done, he went to the back to clear the rear. I could have kicked myself for not realising he might do something like this. When he had cleared the rear window I was, in fact, visible to him, so I just froze turning my face away, that way making it harder for him to detect a human form crouched in the back of his van. Thank fuck he never stared right into the rear and just carried on whistling quietly as he came round to the front driver's door. As Victor opened it, I felt the chill of the morning gust into the van as he positioned his ass on the seat. I was about to make my move when he unexpectedly moved forward with a rag in his hand to wipe the condensation from the inside of the window screen. This only took him a minute or so to do and after finishing, he sat back. I was within an arm's length of him and as I rose from my crouched position, I quickly put my left arm tightly round his neck, tight enough to cut off his air supply. Victor made a small screeching noise as he found himself pinned in his seat and then he started to struggle. Instantly with my right hand, which had the chiv held in it, I thrust it hard in an upward motion straight into the back of his neck and on into Victor's brain, twisting and turning the chiv violently. He had tightly gripped my left arm with both of his hands as I held him in his seat and when the chiv entered his brain, they dropped to his lap. That's when I knew Victor was dead and the job was done.

I got out of the van silently and quickly made my way to a car and then drove to another vehicle I had parked up earlier that day. It was there that I changed into fresh clothes and left the other car in a long stay car park with the keys in it. The reason the keys were left in it was that it would be nicked within twenty-four hours and that way it would have all types of D.N.A. all over it. My hope was that joy riders would nick it because they would probably end up putting a match to it after they had finished. So, in a way, it was a way of covering my tracks and cause some confusion if the car ever got connected with Victor's death.

Chapter Two

'Mother's Revenge'

My thirteenth hit was different from all of the others. My instructions were more specific this time. I had always decided the way of ending my targets' lives. Whether it was by gun, knife or strangulation, I always had the choice of how they died. When I got the call from my source, she spoke to me a lot more intently than usual. The reason was that my next target was to die in a particularly nasty way. I had always carried out my work in a quick, painless and efficient manner. But on this one my target was to be tortured over a forty-eight hour period in a way which would turn the guts of any so-called cold blooded killer. I had never questioned the reason for a hit before, but on this one I did.

'Why?' I asked.

My contact said: 'It is none of your business Jack.'

I reacted angrily to her talking to me like that and roared: 'None of my fucking business Sue!? It's not you having to slowly kill someone is it? If you want me to do this one then you'd best start coming up with an answer to my question or I walk, you got that?'

I was now getting irate with this bitch because she had a way of speaking down to me which pissed me off no end, and if that was not bad enough, she starts giving me the threatening speech. I had named her Sue and the way she spoke to me gave me the impression that she was the one with the strap-on in the dyke relationship.

In a slow and precise way she said to me: 'I have only to make a phone call. Do you understand what I am now saying to you Jack?'

'Yes Sue I understand perfectly, you're talking my language sweetheart. Now you listen to me and you'd better fully understand what I am saying to you. First, don't ever threaten me. Second, if I ask a question then it's obvious there's a good reason and thirdly do you suck cock, or do you drink from the furry cup darling?'

The phone line went dead, so I gathered I had hit a sour note with her. I was not having some fucking go-between bitch talk to me like that. Didn't she know who I was and the amount of respect I warranted? I received a text message a short time later and it said I would be contacted the next day.

I had concerns over this hit, or should I call it torture killing? It wasn't the usual type of contract this Firm would take on. The way they wanted this target sorted told me that this geezer had really upset someone badly. I was not unaccustomed to a bit of torture because I had to use it more times than I can remember whilst working for Fred and the family. It was part of the job description for extortion, but I had never killed anyone like they wanted it done this time. You would have to be really cold-hearted with a touch of psychotic logic added to be able to carry out this type of job.

My phone rang and unsurprisingly Joey was on the other end.

'Listen up Jack and I'll make this chat quick.'

I thought 'here we go', then answered: 'Fire away then Joey.'

'What would you do to someone who kidnapped your son Jack? Took him to a dark dingy basement, raped him, tortured him and then let six other nonces fuck him to death and walk from court on a technicality?'

I was hesitant to answer for a moment because I was quickly weighing up what Joey had said to me. Was he threatening me or was he asking hypothetically?'

'Well Jack, I'm waiting mate, what would you do?'

'I'd kill them all Joey.'

'How Jack?'

'I'd make sure they would suffer in ways that you could not imagine, no matter who they were.'

I emphasised that answer just in case he was threatening me.

'Well Jack this is 'Mother's revenge'; that's what you got as your next target. Have you got any more questions now Jack?'

'No more questions Joey, that's all I needed to hear.'

'Well thank fuck for that, now get on with it will you?'

'I want extra on this one Joey?'

'It's already sorted Jack, double bubble mate.'

'Sweet mate.'

As I was about to hang up he said: 'Oh, by the way Jack, that bird on the blower. She asked me to pass on a message to you: she said that she sucks cock mate and wants you to know that she ain't a muff drinker, so do us all a favour Jack. Try not to question everything mate because she's okay.

Then he hangs up.

I had to smile at Joey's remark over Sue because it was not often this maniac was comical. I now knew that I was dealing with a nonce and already my blood was beginning to boil. I hated those fucked up inhuman scumbags. My opinion is that there should be no prison for these cunts. What should happen with them is this: throw them in a cell with six women who had either been abused or worse still, their children. Tool all the women up with cut throat razors and then leave them to it. Now that's what I would call justice.

Hannah had noticed how quiet and moody I had become since getting this target. It was hard to lie to Han because she was as streetwise as I was. She knew me well enough not to keep on at me though and just let me have the space I needed.

Rubin Peacock was his name; a habitual sex offender who had several convictions along with four related prison sentences. Had this cunt learnt his lesson? Had he fuck? The info I received later on this piece of shit was thorough. I think the reason for so much detail was by design because it was meant to get me in that frame of mind so as to make sure Rubin really suffered; a bit like a red flag to a bull. All who knew me personally knew of my deep hatred for sex offenders because I had been attacked as a kid in a young offender's prison by two nonce screws. Those bastards that tried to fuck me paid dearly for thinking I was easy meat. It cost me an extra two years on my sentence but it was worth every day. Most of that extra time was served in solitary confinement because I kept chinning screws after that. From there on I developed an overwhelming hatred for nonces. Their actions made me feel physically sick; sick to the point that I couldn't read newspaper stories or watch TV reports on sex cases, especially if they involved kids.

So now I had the answer to my original question to Sue. I knew that this job was a form of revenge. I was now able to apply the type of justice all normal people would secretly want for degenerate, shit-eating scum like Rubin Peacock. My conscience was very clear but my thoughts regarding how I was going to deal with the cunt were very dark. I have an ingenious imagination when it comes to hurting someone, especially a nonce. I had decided on a torture plan once I had possession of Rubin and believe me when I say that he was going to suffer very badly. I was about to take this pig to the point where he would want me to kill him.

There were three possible places in Rubin's daily routine where I could nab him. The safest one was when he got into his car which was parked up in his garage. His routine was to leave his house for work at six thirty in the morning. I had only watched this piece of shit for three days before deciding to grab him. Normally I would want to watch my target for three to four weeks before making my move, but with Rubin I had a deep, almost personal anger and desire to kill him slowly as soon as possible. I even justified my hasty thinking by convincing myself that I should act now before my anger subsided because I might not inflict as much damage if I left it any longer.

Grabbing Rubin wasn't a problem. I just waited inside his double garage and when he entered, I grabbed him and shoved a syringe full of diazepam into his neck; just enough to put him asleep for a few hours. Then I transported him to an empty lock-up in the back of an old truck. The location of the lock-up was perfect because it was situated under a railway bridge between its arches. It was a place where his screams could not be heard because the noise from the overhead line could be deafening.

I had tied and gagged Rubin with rubber-backed tape and as I dragged him out of the truck, I purposely let his head bounce off the rear step of the van and onto the concrete floor. The thud of his head hitting the floor was loud and I grew concerned that he might be brain damaged when he came round from the drug. After all, I wanted him to be aware of what was about to happen to him. He had to know what pain was all about and he had to realise that the actions he inflicted on his victims were not fucking acceptable to those of us who care for those poor little mites.

Rubin came round finding himself tied to a large, old plastic-covered twelve seat dining table still gagged. His eyes were like saucers full of fear as the sedative wore off and he began to become aware of his situation. I had tied Rubin naked in a spread eagle position making his body fully exposed. I wore a *Scream* character mask, but not to protect my identity because he was going to die anyway. I wore it to put more fear into him. I had on the usual disposable paper overalls and was completely naked underneath because there was going to be a lot of blood and I had no intention of getting any splashes on my clothes. Rubin was watching me with those saucer shaped eyes as I moved around the dimly-lit room placing all types of implements either side of him.

He kept trying to talk to me but he could only make muffled grunts and groans because of the gag. Then he would panic and try and struggle to free himself, but the rubber-backed tape would expand and retract with each movement of his body, making it impossible to loosen his bonds.

I started off by playing mind games with him.

I asked him: 'Do you know why you're here Mr. Peacock?'

He tried his hardest to answer, but it was impossible to get a coherent word from him.

'Well speak up!' I screamed.

He tried to answer again only this time he went purple with frustration. I made it worse by placing a wood saw and a hammer next to him on a metal top hospital trolley.

I said with a touch of sarcasm: 'You don't look too well Rubin. Seem a bit off colour. Would you like a cigarette? Then we can talk about your predicament; how's that sound?'

His eyes lit up as he eagerly nodded his head in agreement.

'Filter tipped okay for you Rubin?'

Again he nodded his head and grunted a 'yes' as I was opening the packet of fags. As I undid the cellophane wrapper, I glanced at him and jokily said: 'These things will be the death of me Rubin. I'm trying to cut down myself, how about you? Are you trying to quit as well?'

Again he nodded and grunted.

I opened the packet, took my mask off and lit one up, taking a long drag which made the tip red hot. I then moved over to him and pulled a tube of super glue from my overall pocket. Ironically, his eyes were *glued* to me as he could now see the face behind the mask. I looked down at him lying there helpless as I undid the tube top and then squeezed the contents over his hairy chest. I shuddered at the thought of what he must have done to his poor helpless victims and whether he was now feeling any remorse, but it wouldn't have mattered to me if he had because it was far too late for this maggot.

His eyes were now going around in his head like a washing machine on full spin as I put the lighted cigarette onto the glue on his chest. It took two to three seconds till his body jolted into spasm as the pain of the burning fag kicked in. I took a step back from him and continued to light each one of the remaining nineteen fags and then, except for one, placed them on the glue. The room began to smell toxic as the fag tips melted the glue. Then came the smell of burning hair as his chest hair started to singe and fizzle. I sat back in a chair watching this piece of shit scream and thrash about as the cigarettes burnt into his flesh. Tears of pain were running down his face and he pissed himself, soaking my feet. I jumped up from the chair and shouted at him: 'You dirty bastard.'

I then walked over to him and pushed my lighted cigarette straight into his left ear. As I twisted it, his whole body jolted as his muffled screams became hysterical. I looked at him square in the eyes and said to him:

'I'm going to make you suffer like you could never imagine. And by suffering I mean that I am going to torture you slowly until you die an agonising death. Does any of that ring a bell with you Rubin?'

I don't think Rubin heard much of what I was saying to him because the fags had now burnt about half way down on his chest leaving huge watery blisters behind them. Rubin was now going into shock. I decided to sit back and wait for the cigarettes to burn themselves out before making my next move on this piece of smouldering meat.

I had prepared to stay at this lock-up until my task was done. I had told Hannah that I would be away on business for the next couple of days. She would always give me that lovingly concerned look when I left for any business. It was as if she knew what I was up to, but true to form, she never said anything except: 'Come back home safe Jack because we both love and need you.'

I would always say as I left for work: 'Of course I will sweetheart. I won't be long.'

Rubin was whimpering and muttering behind his gag as I checked the damage of the fags. His chest now looked like a pizza topping what with the puss oozing from line after line of blisters. He was sweating profusely and every vein in his body was prominent. I then threw a bucket of ice cold water over him. The water seemed to give him pain relief and his face changed from a painful screwed up look to a look of release similar to orgasm.

I let him have five minutes of relief and then went back to business. This time I was going to administer some plastic surgery by giving him a nose job. First I pulled a bag of ice from a cool box and placed it on his face. Instantly, Rubin started to move his head side to side. I grabbed Rubin's burnt ear and twisted it unmercifully. He went as stiff as a board as I ordered him to stop struggling and let the ice do its job. He just lay there with the bag of ice on his face. There was cold condensation running down the sides of the bag onto his face and into his burnt ear. This must have felt good for him because his ear would have been burning like hell.

My reason for putting the ice on his face was to numb it to congeal the blood in that area. I put a CD on and played the same track by the 70's group *Stealer's Wheel* titled *'Stuck in the Middle with You'* which was used in the Quinton Tarantino movie *Reservoir Dogs*. If he had seen the movie then he would know what the song represented: violent and sadistic torture. After ten minutes with the CD on repeat play, I started to go to work on

Rubin. I removed the ice pack and our eyes met. Mine were full of determined hatred and his were full of fear; a perfect combination for someone like me in this business. I leaned over to grab a pair of pliers from the trolley. Rubin's eyes never left mine and his thinking was probably 'What the fuck is he going to do now?'

As I picked them up, I smashed him straight in his jaw leaving him stunned. I leaned over him and took a Stanley knife from the cupboard top on the other side of him and then used the pliers to grip the end of his nose. I squeezed very tightly; he began to scream and his eyes crossed as he desperately tried to focus on his nose. It was then that I brought the Stanley blade down and across his face and sliced three quarters of his nose off. I then raised and waved it from side to side in front of him with a smile on my face. The blood was minimal because of the clean slice of the blade and the pain he felt was not that bad because his face was numb from the ice. The shock of seeing his own nose being waved about in front of him was what I was after, and that made him pass out. While he was out cold I pushed two McDonald's milkshake straws into the two holes which now passed for a nose. This was to stop any blood running back down his throat choking him to death. I didn't want the cunt dying on me; well not just yet. I had another forty-two hours with this bag of shit.

Next, I placed an iron poker on a two ring gas burner. This implement was to be part of the next stage of Rubin's termination. I turned the music off and looked at Rubin as he lay unconscious. There was a whistling sound coming from the two inserted straws. The blood was now beginning to flow around the wound as the numbing from the ice started to wear off and his blood began to warm up. I knew that as soon as Rubin came-to, the blood would flow even more because he would be back in a state of panic, and panic equals increased heart rate. I lifted the poker from the gas burner. The tip was glowing red; I then used it to carefully cauterize his exposed blood vessels. In an amateurish way I managed to seal and stop most of the bleeding before Rubin woke from his pain-induced blackout.

Rubin went into spasm as soon as his eyes opened. As the smell of his burning flesh had filled the room, it left an overwhelmingly putrid taste in the air. Lucky for Rubin, he passed out again as I hurriedly ran to the toilet to spew my guts up. Since that day I have never eaten meat because that experience was enough to turn me vegetarian. I realised that there could be big problems with keeping Rubin's airways clear, especially with him being gagged. I then decided that if I was to keep this piece of shit alive for a set amount of time, then I would have to remove his gag so he would be able to breathe through his mouth, which then left him able to scream his fucking head off with the pain I was administrating. I knew I had him in a safe location with not many people about, but this fucker would be high pitched pretty soon and I couldn't take any chances.

Rubin was still unconscious as I removed the gag. I picked up the bloodied pliers which still had the remains of his nose stuck between their jaws. I shook the tool until the squashed flesh fell to the floor and with my other hand, I clenched his jaw tightly to open his mouth wide. I gripped the tip of his tongue with the pliers and pulled it out of his mouth as far as it would come and then forcefully sliced at the base with a blade until it came away with the pliers. There was a gush of blood that I quickly stopped by pushing the still hot poker onto the severed stump. The smell was unbearable as his blood began to sizzle and the flesh burnt and fused.

Rubin had not moved or twitched during this procedure and once the bleeding was under control, I checked to see if he was still breathing. I was making a right mess of this and the way things were going, the poor old bastard would be dead before long. There's only so much the body can take and his was getting a pounding. So now I would have to ease up on him to make sure he went the distance. I didn't like this job one bit; it wasn't like the bits of torture I had inflicted before on others, but I had to keep focused on what Rubin represented and had done.

I went into the office of the lock-up and pulled out my thermos flask and poured myself a brew. As I sat watching this piece of messed up shit lie unconscious on the table, he seemed almost content as his breathing was near on normal, apart from the gurgling sound coming from what was left of his nose. My cell phone rang and the number was showing up as my contact, Sue. I thought to myself, 'why the fuck is she calling me?' because she would know I was busy with Rubin.

'Hello Sue, don't you know it's rude to phone me when I'm working?'

'Hello Jack.' said Joey.

'*Joey*? What the fuck do you want? I'm busy mate.'

'That's good to hear Jack. Is the fucker still alive?'

I looked back over my shoulder at Rubin on the table.

'Just about. I've had to ease up on the cunt otherwise he could be dead by morning.'

'Jack, listen to me mate, there's been a change of plan.'

'Change of plan? What the fuck do you mean by that?'

'Don't do no more to him Jack.'

'Why's that?'

'It seems that the mother and auntie want to finish the nonce off themselves.'

'So where does that leave me?'

'Well your job is over. You're still on the same whack so I want you to go home and return in the morning. Then take what's left of the cunt down to Fred's pig farm in Canterbury and feed him to the pigs.'

I felt a sense of relief at being told that because my stomach didn't like this job at all. My thoughts were now on Rubin because he was about to be finished off by two very angry, pissed off, bereaved women and I could only imagine what they had in store for him. I was wondering what state he would be in by the time I arrived back in the morning to pick him up – whatever was left of the fucker.

'Okay mate, no problem.'

'One more thing Jack, bring some heavy duty bin liners and make sure the place goes up in smoke, okay?'

'Okay Joey, I'll sort it.'

'Good man Jack. See you soon.'

I thought: 'Not if I can help it.' I disliked Joey, the creepy motherfucker.

I made my way back home thinking over what had happened during the course of the day. I was beginning to comprehend what I had actually done to Rubin. My thoughts were getting complicated which usually meant trouble for me. I was doing my utmost to rationalise it all and treat it as strictly business because Rubin was a sexual predator. He deserved all he got, but there was something deeper that was bothering me. It was an underlying feeling of discomfort and fear, and over the years, I had trained myself to ignore fear. I have done many nasty things in my lifetime and I have always managed to clear my conscience during and after I did the business. But I had never before been in this type of situation where I was slowly torturing someone to death. I could justify what Rubin had coming to him, but when it came to inflicting his given punishment, I found that my emotions were being triggered. I definitely didn't enjoy torturing Rubin the way I was instructed. I'd sooner have treble tapped him; one bullet in the bollocks then five minutes later another one in the liver and finally one in the forehead – job done. This torturing stuff was never my cup of tea and apart from that, it was fucking messy.

Here, I was now thinking of things that normally would not bother me. My gut feeling kept coming into play and when that happens, I have to take notice because I have been saved many times due to that intuition. It feels as if something is not quite right, and what I usually do, is stop what I'm doing and just feel the feeling. Then I either change what I'm about to do or don't do it at all, and nine times out of ten, I've been right. On this piece of work it was different; perhaps it was telling me that it was time for me to get out of this business. Perhaps it was telling me I was no longer that cold-hearted murdering bastard anymore.

Hannah was surprised to see me home early and greeted me with a big cuddle and kiss. I could hear Jack Junior in the other room and went in to see him while Han made me a cup of tea. I sat down on the sofa and picked up Junior, sat him on my knee and just gazed into his big blue eyes. I thought to myself about how I loved him so much and how lucky I was to have him. These feelings of gratitude were something I rarely felt and when Han handed me my tea I looked up at her and just said:

'I love you babe.'

Han giggled and said: 'I know you do sweetheart.'

I went on to tell her how lucky I was to have them both and that I shouldn't take all that I love for granted.

'What's all this about Jack? Why have you gone all soppy on me?'

'I'm not going soppy Han, I'm just feeling grateful for what I have; that's all.'

She came and sat next to me and leaned her head on my shoulder. I was still holding Junior when she said: 'What's happened Jack?'

I paused for a few seconds and replied: 'I've just had an unusual and stressful day babe.'

She lifted her head up and looked into my eyes: 'Do you want to talk about it darling? It helps you know.'

I would have loved to have sat there and poured my feelings out to her but I knew I couldn't. How the fuck could I tell her?

'Oh Han it's just that I've tortured a nonce half to death and its having an effect on me.'

I just told her that I had a bit of a bad day and was glad to be home.

'Are you in trouble?'

'No babe, everything's okay, it's just been one of those days, that's all. And I'm dead tired. So do me a favour sweetheart and cook us something to eat while I take a bath will you?'

I would always do what I call 'shut down' when something was getting to me. I would go over it in my head till I came up with a solution, but this problem was one that I had never felt or dealt with before. In my line of business it was not possible for me to have a counsellor who I could have gone to and shared my feelings and thoughts with. If it was possible, I would have probably had to whack them as soon as I had unloaded my shit, so I had to be my own counsellor.

I had a restless sleep that night; it didn't help knowing that I had to return to the lock-up in the morning and the sort of mess I was likely to walk into. Han was up early with Junior and brought me a cup of tea.

'Are working today Jack?'

'Yeah sweetheart; got to finish something off and take a run down to Fred's farm.'

She said excitedly: 'Can Junior and me come along for the ride? It's been ages since we've been out to the sticks.'

'Not this time babe because I'm on business. Let's go down to Margate or Laysdown this weekend and make a couple of days of it. I think all three of us need a break.'

Her eyes lit up and she said sweetly. 'Ohhhh babe, that would be so nice. We could have a picnic and a paddle in the sea.'

Hannah never asked for much and she was very easy to please ever since she had her operation. She did tell me many times that she treasured every day of life since. Even if the weather was pissing down, she would still be smiling and I admired her for that.

'Put the kettle on sweetheart while I take a shower. By the way, have we got any strong bin liners?'

'Bin liners? What do you want with them?'

I just looked at Han and took a deep breath.

'Sorry darling I didn't mean to pry. How many do you need?'

After a quick calculation I replied: 'About a dozen babe.'

While taking my shower I went into deep reflection again and that gut feeling of mine returned to the surface. I tried to put it down to not having much sleep. But if truth be known, I was feeling a bit worried, even if I didn't want to admit it. As a kid I had always been afraid because I had been bullied up to the age of ten. An old time villain took pity on me and showed me his ways of fighting back. Once I learnt all he had to offer, I became a formidable character and quickly passed on my given knowledge to those that I chose as my mates. That became my introduction to gangs and crime and with that, came all sorts of illegal skulduggery.

The only real fear I've ever felt since, was when my son George fell ill and nearly died with kidney failure. That was the only time that I had ever felt frightened enough to pray. That's why I could relate to seeing Han on her knees just before her operation. This feeling was different though. I just could not nail it or find out the root cause of what was happening to me.

I got a taxi to the lock-up carrying a few tools in my bag along with my overalls and the bin liners. I was dreading what I was about to walk into because when those two bereaved pissed off women got their hands on the nonce that was responsible for the torture and death of their loved one, then only my imagination could prepare me. So I thought of the worst possible scenario to help me cope with the situation. As I entered the lock-up there was a strong smell of petrol and burnt meat in the air. I walked around the truck to see if there was a fuel leak because the smell was so strong. It was then that I came across what was left of Rubin. I noticed he was still tied to the table and as I got alongside him, I realised that the entire floor around the table was covered in blood and guts. Immediately my stomach started to churn and I began to heave. I rushed to the toilet to spew up. Fortunately I had decided to skip breakfast that morning because it would have ended up down the loo. I had mentally prepared myself for the sort of condition that Rubin would be in on entering the lock-up. Unfortunately it was not enough because the sight I came across was like something out of *The Texas Chainsaw Massacre*.

Rubin had been butchered beyond recognition. The first thing I noticed was that there was a huge hole where his dick and balls once were. These women had actually cut his whole package out of his body in a circular hacking cut. By briefly examining the cuts, it appeared they had used something like a blunt machete or a butcher's meat cleaver. Lying amongst the pool of blood were his fingers and toes; they had been hacked off and scattered about the concrete floor. Then I found what resembled ears, and by the condition of them, it must have taken a few swings to get them off because the side of Rubin's skull was still attached to them leaving his brain partially exposed. I found his dick and bollocks stuffed in the back of his throat. They had even poured petrol all over him, probably during the early stages of his demise, to either cause him to panic by threatening to set him alight, or to make his wounds hurt even more. But in the case of these girls, it was probably both.

They had really gone to town on this piece of shit. I only wished that what I was seeing could be communicated to would-be sex offenders because if it were possible, then I would definitely think it would make the sick bastards have second thoughts before thinking about what they were about to do. A good deterrent don't you think?

Both eyes had been gouged out and he had been stabbed hundreds of times, probably done at the point of near death; in a mad frenzy to finish the sick cunt off. This bastard must have suffered big time and I couldn't even imagine what sort of agony he had felt. But it was fair to say that justice was served – *South London style.'*

I opened up my bag and put my overalls on. I then pulled out a sharpened meat cleaver and a hacksaw and started to chop and saw away at his legs just below the knee caps. This was with the intention of cutting him up into manageable pieces so that the pigs could lunch on him. I used the hacksaw to cut through the bone and tendons. You would be surprised how tough the human body is and cutting this scum bag up into small pieces was hard work.

After two hours I had completed my task and poor old Rubin was now manageable and put into a dozen bin liners and thrown into the back of the truck which had been covered in plastic sheeting from the floor to the ceiling. I was surprised how heavy some of the chunks were, especially his head, which weighed about the same as a junior bowling ball. After Rubin was all packed away, I started to clear the area of any bone fragments or the odd toe or finger. I pulled the toilet bowl away from the floor because I didn't want to leave that behind. I had been spewing my guts up down it a few times and it was the only place that my DNA could survive the fire I was about to start; so that went into the back of the van as well. Once I was satisfied that the place was clean, I picked up a 25 litre jerry can of petrol and started to pour it all over the lock-up. To finish off, I taped a battery cooker igniter, complete with a timer, to a separate five litre can of petrol. This would be the device that would start the inferno. I set it so that it would give me ample time to finish the job at the farm and be tucked up in bed at home when the petrol bomb exploded. The chances of early detection of the fire would be minimal because of the location and time.

The relief I felt when I left that lock-up was overwhelming. The sunlight was bright to my eyes and warm to my skin and the fresh air smelt sweet. It was a lot better than the awful stench of death and fumes that lingered inside.

As I travelled along the A2 towards Canterbury, I began to feel less nauseous and my appetite was beginning to return. I pulled over into one of those lay-by caravan diners and tucked into a cheese sandwich and a mug of tea. By now I was only a short distance from Fred's farm and a load of hungry pigs. I had been told that if you starve a pig for three to four days, it will eat half its own body weight on its first serving because they are greedy bastards. Hence the saying 'eats like a pig'. Pigs will eat anything, including humans. They will consume everything except teeth. It was my job to remove them from Rubin's skull and I didn't fancy undertaking that task one bit.

When I drove up the potholed track way leading to the rear of the farm, I noticed a welcoming party of three geezers all dressed in the usual white coloured disposable overalls. Once I reached them, I was greeted by Fred's 'yes man': a bloke called Myers who was an upper middle class type with a posh accent and plenty of chat to go with it. He was also a shrewd and clever bastard and had been on the Firm for about ten years. Fair play to him: he got himself fast-tracked to the white collar sector of the Firm. Myers mainly gave Fred sound advice on delicate business matters. He was also an expert negotiator when it came down to dealing with other Firms, mainly those from over the East side of the river.

'You're late Jack.' was how I was greeted.

I replied: 'It took longer than I thought Myers, now where do you want this load?'

'Take it round the back of the barn dear boy where you will see the pig sty.

I slowly drove around the back of the barn to where the pigs were and once they were in sight, they all came rushing out of their shelter in anticipation of getting some grub. I got out of the cab and began unlocking the back of the truck where Rubin was being stored. Myers came around to the back of the truck where I was with his two men and asked me if the job went okay.

'I got the job done if that's what you mean mate, but it was a fucking nightmare carrying it out.'

'Why's that Jack. Could your stomach not take it?' He started to snigger.

I just gave him my stare and said nothing as I opened the back doors of the truck. Myers', whose snigger turned into laughter when he clapped his eyes on the contents, then loudly said.

'What the hell?!'

I looked at him then turned my head to see what he found so amusing.

'Why on earth, have you got a toilet bowl amongst that lot Jack?'

I wasn't about to tell him that I had had been spewing my guts up down it, so I told him that I had been using it to piss, so therefore, I didn't want it left behind just in case of evidence.

'Good thinking. That's what I like about you; you're always one step in front dear fellow. Leave it with me and I will get one of the boys to dispose of it. But if you do not mind me saying, the next time you do a job of this nature, my advice would be that it would be wise to use a plastic bottle old sport.'

Myers had a point and I could have kicked myself because I always thought I was a clever bastard when covering my tracks. I ate a bit of humble pie, took on board his advice, and changed the subject back to the job in hand.

I said: 'Where do want this lot?' pointing to the bin liners.

Myers gave the other two geezers the nod and they jumped inside and started to unload the bags.

I explained to him that the head was in one of the bags on its own, complete with the teeth. Myers instructed one of the geezers in the back to find it and to put it to one side.

We all carried a few bags each to the edge of the sty and the pigs could sense that feeding time was about to commence because they were squealing and running about in a frenzy. Myers picked up a long-handled axe and wrapped a rag around the head, then said to one of the other two:

'Pass me the head will you please Bill?'

Bill threw the head, which was still wrapped in the bag, and it landed at Myers' feet. He moved the bag into position with his foot, took one step backwards and raised the axe above his head. I could guess what was about to happen when Myers brought the blunt side of the axe head crashing down onto the bag. There was a loud crack as the axe hit its target. The rag had stopped the bin liner splitting and you could tell that from that blow, the skull had been cracked open like a walnut. He carried out the same procedure four or five times until the bag was near on flat. Myers spoke almost jokingly: 'Open it up Bill and collect the teeth and no nicking any for the tooth fairy okay?'

Myers and his two cronies started laughing but I was more impressed with the method they used to get the teeth out of the skull. I thought I would have had to pull them out with a pair of pliers, and the way my guts had been performing, I'd probably have spewed up my now half-digested cheese sandwich.

‘What is the matter Jack? Are you feeling a bit peaky? You don’t look too good.’

Trying to brush off his comment, I said: ‘I’m okay mate, I’ve just never seen that technique used before.’

I had to smile when he answered: ‘That’s what we call our den-plan service Jack.’

One of Myer’s cronies emptied the bags with the remains of Rubin into a wheelbarrow. He now resembled a train wreck victim that had been caught under the wheels. Myers walked over to the wheelbarrow and inspected the remains.

‘Bloody nice job Jack. Usually, when I get them I end up having to cut the buggers up myself because the lazy sods cannot be assed to cut them into joint sizes.

‘Took me over two hours to get that cunt down to that size Myers and, to be honest mate, it was fucking hard work’.

‘I know only too well Jack, but I have learnt that it is always best to use a chainsaw; that way it only takes five minutes.’

‘I’ll bear that in mind next time.’

Myers had made a good point because it would have been far quicker.

What I saw next was revolting. Bill had retrieved all the teeth from the skull and was emptying the remains of Rubin’s head, which was now smashed into small pieces, into the pig trough. The pigs went berserk as the remains hit the already licked-clean troth. They were fighting each other to get a piece of his head and brain and the sound of them crunching bone was sickening to hear. Myers came and stood next to me as my eyes were transfixed by this awful sight.

‘Bon appétit. They don’t hang about do they Jack?’

‘Fucking right they don’t. It’s gross mate; doing this job has turned me vegetarian.’

Myers pissed himself laughing after my remark but then his face turned serious and he said: ‘It is always wise to get rid of the head first Jack because that is the hardest part to do away with.’

I asked: ‘How long have this lot been starved for?’

‘Five days old boy and believe me, they are famished. There will be nothing left of our dear friend here in half an hour and when he has been all gobbled up, they will then eat their own excrement, getting rid of every trace’

‘Fucking ingenious Myers, I’ll give you that.’

His droll reply was: ‘It is all part of the food chain Jack.’

I looked right at him and said: ‘Fucking food chain? I’ll never buy a bit of pork from this side of the country again.'

All of us then started to laugh as the last bit of Rubin was fed to the pigs.

I may have been laughing, but I didn't feel amused or happy. I had learnt something that day: I was not like Myers and his pals. They, especially Myers, handled that situation as if it was a normal part of their day's work. They showed no sign of revulsion for performing this kind of task. For them, it was just another job of work on Fred's pig farm. I knew then that that gut instinct of mine was showing itself to me again and this time I could nail it. I had come to the conclusion that I was not cut out for this business any longer and it was that which had been bothering me mentally.

What I couldn't fathom out was why it was happening now. Why didn't I have these thoughts before? Did it mean that I was turning soft? Perish the thought if that was the case because I could be in deep trouble with the Firm. This new line of work was an alternative to a bullet in my head and I had given my word which meant there was no going back.

Chapter Three

'Confession'

That weekend, as promised, we went down to Laysdown to have a well-earned family-orientated couple of days. At first, my thoughts were far away from the Freds and Sues of my world. I had purposely left my cell phone at home because I was in dire need of some family time after the Rubin affair.

Hannah was so happy and smiled all weekend. We had rented out a nice house with a separate indoor heated swimming pool. Han was determined to get Jack Junior used to the water and spent hours in there with him teaching him how to swim. I spent a lot of time just gazing at the two of them thrashing about and having fun in the pool. Again those thoughts of gratitude would return, but always accompanied by that uneasy feeling in my gut. This time I knew what was going on and I decided I had to do something about it when I got back to South London.

I made sure that Han and Junior had a great weekend because it was hard for me to turn off sometimes and it showed. I had always been a quiet geezer, never a loud mouth or party animal. On top of this, I was unfortunate enough to have a natural expression of '*Don't fuck with me.*' on my face when I was in deep thought. Some people who didn't know me very well would think of it as a look that told them I was someone they should keep at arm's length. Come to that, even those that *did* know me would do the same, which meant I could not be read. I had a temper and believe me it could be bad, but it took time to wind me up. Han would always leave me to it when I went into think mode. I suppose in her way, it was much safer to leave me to it because she knew I hated to be asked if I was okay. To put it in a nutshell, I was unpredictable to most people, and those that did know of my temper, knew it was much safer to keep their distance.

While we were driving back to London, I noticed that Hannah was very quiet; just staring out of the window. Junior was in the back fast asleep and she could see I had that buttoned-up look on my face. Han lit a cigarette, passed it to me, and said: 'Jack, please don't bite my head off darling, but I've noticed you have that look on your face.'

I butted in on her when she said: 'Hear me out Jack because I need to get this off my chest.'

'Go on then Han, spit it out.' I said

'Jack, I've known you long enough to know that something is bothering you. I have never pried into your business dealings because I know that the less that I know is better for me and Junior, but you're giving off some worrying vibes sweetheart, and I'm getting a bit worried about you.'

'Look Han, there's fuck all bothering me babe, I've just got a lot on that's all.'

Hannah moved her posture in her seat so that she was looking at me side on and then said: 'Look Jack I'm not stupid. What happened to you being retired and spending more time with Junior and me?'

'We've just had a weekend together haven't we?'

'Yes we did, but Jack wasn't there.'

'What do you mean I wasn't there? Where the hell was I then?'

'I don't know. You might have thought you were with us, but all's I saw was a vacant Jack on auto pilot.'

There was no pulling the wool over Han's eyes. As I've already said, she was a very streetwise woman who could pick up on my vibes, so she knew I was bullshitting her when I said I was okay.

'Look babe I *am* retired but I still have to do some part-time work for the Firm and it's that which has been bothering me.'

'Do you want to talk about it?'

'No Hannah I don't.'

'Does that mean you're going to be a miserable sod all the time then?'

I gave Han the look, but she just stared back at me and said in a caring almost tender, way: 'Jack I'll be honest with you and I hope you will be with me. Over the last few weeks you have been acting strangely and I am getting very worried about Junior and me. You have been talking in your sleep about all types of things and I have never known you to do that before. I know there's a problem with you and it's not just a small one either. Please Jack, give me some peace and sort it out if you're not going to tell me because I've had enough of worrying.'

I knew Han was right but I could not tell her what was on my mind. I didn't want to lie to her either because, as I said, she knew what bullshit was.

'Okay babe I'll sort it out as soon as I get back.'

Han gave me her look which meant *'don't fuck me about'*, then said:

'Do you promise Jack?'

'I promise sweetheart.'

Once we arrived home I decided to go down the pub for a drink and have a bit of time away from Han to collect my thoughts. There were no villains in my local, just ordinary working-class people. Most of them knew that I was a heavy but treated me no different. I had known many of them since I was a kid. It was while I was in the pub that our local priest came in for his usual. His name was Father Malone; he was in his mid fifties, Irish with snow white hair and a real diamond of a man. He loved his *Jamieson's Whiskey* and you could always find him propped up against the bar in the evenings.

'Hello Jack and how are we tonight?'

'I'm fine Father and how about you?'

'I am very well and how is that good lady of yours and Jack Junior keeping?'

'They're okay Father.'

'That's good to hear Jack. Now, when are you going to have that son of yours baptised?'

'Soon Father, soon.'

'And is he going to be Catholic?'

'Of course.'

'Is Hannah happy with having young Jack baptised as a Catholic?'

Hannah and I had discussed Junior's christening just after his birth and where Han was a Protestant and me a Catholic, we had a few heated discussions regarding which faith he was to be given, but in the end I got my own way.

'Yeah Father she's happy going with R.C.'

'Well done Jack, and will I see you at church soon?'

I had been baptised a Catholic and was half Irish. My Father came from Dublin and my Mother came from Deptford, South London. Mum converted to the Catholic faith so she could get married to my Dad and they both made me go to church as a kid until I was confirmed. As soon as I had my confirmation, I stopped going – apart from when I had been banged up in the nick. Then I only used it as an excuse to get out of my cell. Basically, I class myself as a lapsed Catholic.

'I've been busy Father, but I'll get there soon.'

We went on to have a good chat and I kept up with him with the whiskeys. It felt good to chat with him and I found myself talking to him rather deeply about my feelings. He obviously sussed that there was something wrong with me and asked me to come to the church the next day to sort out a date for the christening and make confession. Where I'd had a few drinks down me, I agreed.

That night I slept like a log and was up early enough to change and feed Junior. By helping out with the boy, I could give my Han a well-earned lie-in. When she got breakfast in bed she said in surprise:

'Wow, that chat we had yesterday must have done something to you.'

I just smiled, and as a joke, told her not to expect this every morning, at which point she threw a piece of toast at me as I was leaving the bedroom. Han was a great laugh and had a fantastic personality, especially in the mornings and I loved her to bits.

My first marriage was a good one but I let my work affect it which put a lot of pressure on my wife. In the end, she called it a day and divorced me. But now I was getting a second bite of the cherry with Hannah. Even though she was a lot younger than me, she had the mindset and character of a much wiser, older woman and would often give me good sound advice, even when I didn't want it. When Han came into the kitchen she asked me what I had planned for the day. I knew she was pumping me because I had said the day before that I was going to sort out my little problem.

'I'm off to see Father Malone.'

Han choked on her cigarette and said: 'Is it that bad Jack? Or have you found religion?'

I had to laugh at her remark and told her that I was going along to sort out Junior's christening.

'That's great darling, so when were you going to involve me then?'

'I didn't know myself until last night babe.'

'What happened last night?'

I went on to tell her of my chat with Father Malone and that he was being very persistent about Junior getting baptised.

I left Han and Junior at the house and made my way to St Mary Church. Once there I went around back to the vestry where Father Malone was expecting me.

'Well, well, Jack, praise the Lord.'

I looked at him and wondered what the hell he was going on about.

'Be-Jesus you're a sight for the saints Jack.'

I gave him a confused look and said: 'Why's that Father?'

He smiled and replied in his soft Irish accent; 'To have you walk into my vestry my son; that on its own is a miracle.'

I had to laugh at him as I approached him to shake his hand.

'Come in and let's have a tot of the extra holy water.'

By that remark I knew he was talking about having a whiskey, but I'd had enough from the previous night and declined the offer and stuck to the tea. Once we had made all the arrangements for the christening, Father Malone asked me if I wanted to make confession.

'Sorry Father but I'll have to leave it until another time because I've got a lot on today.'

He wasn't having any of it and said: 'Jack, how long have we known each other?'

'A long time Father.'

'During that time have I ever treated you different from the rest of my flock?'

'Not as far as I know, but what's that got to do with me making confession?'

'How is Fred Jack?'

I thought: 'What the fuck is he going on about, mentioning Fred?'

Softly he said: 'Jack, Jack, Jack, do you really think I don't know what you and the likes of Fred do for an occupation?'

Instantly I went on the defensive and said to him: 'It's all hearsay Father, you should know better than to listen to rumours.'

He let out a huge belt of laughter. I looked at him oddly, thinking maybe he had been on the sauce a bit too much that morning.

'Listen to me Jack; I know more than you think. Do you honestly imagine that you are the only one from the Firm who has sat where you are sitting now?'

I knew he had me and that there was no use denying what I was because this geezer knew probably more about me than I did. I also knew that there were a few of us that had kept ties to the church, but in a quiet and discrete way. Confession with a priest, stayed with the priest; it went no further apart from the Almighty. My thinking was that God already knew what I was and what I had done, so what was the point in confessing it if he already knew? It was obvious other members had been in this seat and that they had probably spilled their guts to him. But with me, I had this useful habit of keeping my mouth shut about the things I got up to. I then had a brainwave and thought for a moment that maybe this could be a good time to unload all my shit to a person who cannot say fuck all to anyone, and at the same time be forgiven, leaving me with a clean slate.

'I accept you know a lot about me Father, but I don't think you would want anything to do with me if I told you half of what has gone on.'

'Let God be the judge on that one Jack.'

'Okay Father you've asked for it. Where do I start?'

He replied with a considerate tone to his voice: 'Why don't you begin where your conscience tells you should start from Jack?'

I sat there thinking to myself: 'What the fuck have I let myself in for here?'

As I looked at Father Malone, he positioned himself so that he was side on to me with his eyes closed and head bowed towards the floor.

'When you're ready Jack.'

I was very anxious and the palms of my hands were now sweating.

'Forgive me Father for I have sinned, it has been over thirty-five years since my last confession…'

I spent the next hour confessing every single wrong deed I could remember, even the murders. At first it was hard for me to talk about the things I had done. I started with the lighter stuff to see what sort of reaction I would get from him. His expression stayed the same as I upped the pace and got even deeper into the dark side of my wrongdoings. I had always thought that there was no hope for me when it came to the Church. The way I looked at it was, because I had done so many bad things throughout my life, God did not have a place for me. I was past redemption with a one-way ticket to the pits of hell. I finally got to the Rubin affair and told him everything, including my feelings of fear and anxiety.

When I finished Father Malone said: 'Your sins are grave indeed my son and it is only right that you should feel this fear and anxiety. Another word for this might be remorse. With remorse must come a desire for change and to make amends for what you've done. I will give you absolution but the rest is up to you.'

Father Malone absolved me of my sins and gave me penance. Then he turned to face me. I still could not see any reaction from him. I thought to myself that he must think I'm just a hideous, murdering bastard, when surprisingly he said to me: 'Well done Jack, I think you are ready for that wee tot now.'

With a sense of relief I answered: 'Make it a large one Father.'

While we sat there supping our whiskey he went on to tell me that because I had confessed to my sins, it did not necessarily mean that I had a clean slate with the man above. I had to want forgiveness and be genuinely sorry for my wrongdoings.

'Are you sorry for your sins Jack?'

I had to think about that question and paused for a moment.

'It's very easy for me to justify my sins Father because it was all strictly business.'

'Forget business Jack and tell me what your heart says?'

'Let's put it this way Father, if I was not in this business with the Firm, then the chances are that I would not have committed a majority of my sins.'

Father Malone paused and closed his eyes as if he was in prayer then he opened them and said: 'You have just found the answer to your problem my son.'

I was now a bit confused and replied: 'What do you mean Father, I've found the answer?'

'You just said it Jack. If you were not working for Fred, then most of what you have just confessed to would never have happened. Am I right?'

It was obvious what he was getting at. What he was saying to me was to get out and away from the Firm.

'I've tried getting out of the Firm when Hannah fell ill but they gave me this so called part-time work to do. If I'm honest Father, I'm not cut out for it. But I'm in a *Catch 22* situation; it's either do the work or end up swimming with the fishes.'

'Jack, I know that Fred is a heartless bastard and that he puts on a show, but you have to make a decision whether you carry on with his Firm and commit more dreadful sins.'

He had a point and I knew at that moment I had to do something about my situation because I truly wanted out.

'Father, do you know what that means?'

He leaned over to me and clasped my hand, then looked me straight in the eyes and spoke in a soft whisper: 'I have a good idea Jack and I know that you can do it.'

'Listen to me Father, even if I did a bunk and set up somewhere else with a dodgy name, they would still eventually find me. And I have Hannah and Junior to look out for.'

'Jack my son; you are a very clever man. God gave you a brain and a conscience and with that you have a choice, so choose wisely.'

I saw something in Father Malone that morning which told me that this old Paddy priest was not as naïve about the business I was mixed up in as I first thought. It was as if he was telling me something without having to be direct and I picked up on it straight away.

'Okay Father I'll have to have a good think about how I'm going to get out. I have to make sure Hannah and Junior are the priority though, whatever the cost.'

Father Malone just smiled at me and said: 'I will pray for you Jack that you make the right decision. Now go and put your thinking head on and pray for our Lord's guidance.'

When I got back into my car I sat at the wheel deep in thought. My mind was not racing as I expected it to be. In fact, I felt quite calm and focussed. My thinking was now in survival mode because if I wanted out of this business, then I might have to go to extreme measures to secure my family's wellbeing so that they came out safe and sound and in one piece.

There were only two ways for me to walk away into the sunset. One would be if we left London and moved to South America or some other place well out of range of Fred and Joey. But then I would have to consider how long my money would last. I had a nice few quid put away in an offshore account, but not enough to keep us going for a lifetime. Then there was Junior's education that had to be considered and that would not come cheap. In fact, the more I thought about it, the whole idea of fleeing was becoming a non-starter. The other way was much easier, but extremely dangerous and would have to be planned with precision. That way would mean that I would have to whack Fred and Joey. I would then have no one to answer to because with those two out of the way the Firm would fragment go bust in no time. There wasn't anyone clever enough in the Firm who could command the respect required to take over Fred. What would probably happen would be that Fred's empire would be carved up between the other London Firms and its crew would start working for new bosses.

This idea was now becoming more appealing to me the more I thought about it. My instinct was telling me it was the best out of the two options.

Chapter Four

'A Way Out'

Over the next few weeks I did a lot of thinking and my thoughts were strictly centred on devising a plan that would get me out of the Firm without any comebacks.

I definitely couldn't afford to be hasty or become reckless with my would-be plan and run the risk of anyone pointing the finger at me. I have always considered myself an intelligent man, even though I'd had little formal education. I had been in this business of crime for many years and had to deal with all types of situations. I was a well trusted member of Fred's Firm and had proved my loyalty many times which made me in their eyes a staunch and sound member who could be trusted. I had got to know how they operated and I knew the whole operation inside and out; from the prostitution rings right up to the overseas drug trafficking business. I had seen and been part of things that only top members were privileged to witness. To be white collar management in Fred's Firm you usually had to be part of his blood line or marry into the family. I wasn't either, but I was still accepted unofficially as one of the family. I was allowed to put my views across when meetings were taking place and I also made important decisions off my own back when Fred or Joey weren't around. Not once over the years had I been looked at twice or doubted and as far as the Firm were concerned, I had a level respect that gave me a certain amount of clout.

I knew everything about Fred and Joey, from where their safe houses were and even what offshore accounts they used. I was trusted with this type of information. I also knew who were our enemies and opposition which gave me another avenue to think about in my quest to get out. Fred was the number one of the business. He was a ruthless man who took no prisoners and his reputation was highly respected in the criminal underworld.

Joey had married himself into the Firm by getting hitched to Fred's daughter, so that made him family. He was a psychotic maniac who dealt with the messy side of the business and would take care of contract killings and any punishments that needed to be handed out. He wasn't what I would call a bright spark because his reputation had only come by the way of the amount of violence he dished out. When Joey was only thirteen, he killed his alcoholic father with an iron bar for battering his mother and got away with just a two year borstal sentence. As such, he was feared by many. However, it was Fred's reputation that carried the most clout and Joey knew it and used it to his own advantage. He would sometimes go over the top when dishing out some of the punishments, but because he was Fred's son in-law, he got away with it and for that, he was a disliked man by a large number of us villains.

Things went very quiet on the job front and I was spending some real quality time with Hannah and Junior. We went to theme parks, zoos and even the circus, and I was adjusting to family life in a big way. In my first marriage we had four kids and during their childhood, I was mainly out of the picture because of my work for the Firm. Most of the time I was on call 24/7 and Fred used me as much as possible simply because I was good at my job. I got results and had earned him a fortune. Bearing in mind that Fred was a greedy selfish bastard, he never considered that I might want some time off to be with my family. My wife at that time accepted it for the first few years because she knew I never had much of a choice. The only good thing about working for Fred was the money; it paid well and we never wanted for anything, except for me being there for the kids. Most nights I wouldn't get home till the early hours when the children were all tucked up, and by the time I got up, they were either at school or at nursery. So after a while, I became a virtual stranger to them. In fact, I could count on the fingers of one hand the number of times I had been there for them on Christmas morning.

So in a way, I was now trying to be a father again; only this time the correct way, and I was really enjoying it. Hannah only ever wanted us to be one happy family and would frequently talk about moving away to the country to start again. South London was becoming a no-go zone and far from the ideal place to bring up a family. My ties to the Firm stopped me from doing what I wanted, even though I was meant to be retired. For instance, they would not agree for me to move too far away. The furthest anyone lived from Fred's HQ was twenty miles away in Kent; that way he had a hold on all who worked for him.

Hannah and I had just got home after a romantic weekend in Brighton when there was a knock on our door. When I opened it there in front of me was Danny, who was a runner for the Firm. Runners were only used when things got a bit naughty and no one was trusting cell phones. That way the message that was delivered was safe and away from prying ears.

'What's up Dan?' I asked.

'There's a meeting. Jack and Fred want you back at the factory pronto!'

I was well pissed off with the way he spoke to me. It was more like an order than a request. He had managed to light the fuse to my temper and as I grabbed him by his lapels, I angrily replied to him: 'Don't you ever 'pronto' me again you fucking gobby little cunt!'

Danny pulled himself free from my grip, backed away and nervously replied: 'Hang on Jack! Take it easy mate; those were Fred's words not mine. I'm only the messenger.'

I calmed down a little and told Danny to come in while I changed into some clean clothes.

'What's it all about then Danny?' I asked.

He replied: 'I think it's all kicked off with those Yardie bastards that Joey was dealing with.'

I had heard through the grapevine that Fred had been persuaded by Joey to do some drug business with the Yardies and now it looked like it had backfired on him. Fred was old school and when it came down to business, he wasn't used to working with the West Indian cartels. He was okay with the Russians and Romanians and the way they did business because it was similar to the way he conducted his own, but the 'Yardies were a different kettle of fish. Yardies have no respect for anyone, not even their own and doing business with them was always very risky. Fred, on the other hand, had so much ego and pride that he believed his infamous reputation would stop any other Firm, including the Yardies, from taking the piss. He was so pig- headed that he wouldn't listen to the warnings and sound advice that was given, prior to him working with them. Instead he took Joey's word that all would be fine; that the Yardies had respect for Fred and his Firm. But the unspoken opinion of most of the Firm was that Joey was a fucking idiot, especially when it came down to doing business. It was my guess that something really bad had happened and now it had to be sorted out.

Hannah realised something was up and came into the bedroom where I was changing.

'What was all that about Jack?'

I quickly responded: 'What's what about Han?'

She put her hands on her hips as if to square up to me and said: 'Why did you shout at Danny? It's not like you to pop him out; what's he done babe?'

I only had to take one look at Hannah to realise that I couldn't bullshit her.

'Danny came round here to pass a message from Fred because it seems that there's a bit of bother going down and Fred needs to see me.'

Han's voice sounded confused when she said: 'I thought you were retired Jack.'

Frustrated, I replied: 'I am fucking retired Han! That's why I bit Danny's head off, so don't ask me anymore questions because I ain't got any answers until I see Fred, okay!'

'Okay calm down. Just be careful sweetheart.'

I realised the way I had spoken to Hannah was a bit harsh and that it had upset her; after all she was only concerned about me.

'I'm sorry babe, it's just that I thought I was away from all this crap and now it seems that I'm not.'

Hannah came over to me and gave me a big hug and said very quietly in my ear: 'Can't we do a bunk and get away from the likes of Fred? 'Cause we'll never see any peace otherwise.'

'I'm working on that one already babe and believe me, I'm not bullshitting you.'

Hannah just smiled at me and walked back out of the room. I knew she was getting worried for me and the last thing I wanted was for her to fret, especially since her illness.

Danny drove me to The Factory, which was the name that we in the Firm used for Fred's office. As I entered Fred's smoke-filled office, I could hardly see through the haze made by the 'white collar' workers of the Firm. There were a dozen of them in all. They were all talking at the same time as they sat at a huge conference table with Fred at one end and Joey at the other. No one noticed me as I made my way to Fred's end until a voice shouted: 'Quiet gentlemen please!'

As silence fell upon the room, all their eyes were transfixed on me as I pulled a chair up right next to where Fred was sitting.

Fred said: 'Thank you all for coming gentlemen.'

My thoughts went back thirty minutes to the way Danny had delivered Fred's message, and here he was sitting there thanking us all for coming as if we had a choice.

I said my hellos to the rest of the lads and then looked at Fred and asked: 'What's up Fred?'

He looked at me then he turned and looked up the table to where Joey was sitting.

'Tell him Joey.'

'Hello Jack it seems we have a little problem with…'

Fred burst right in on Joey's explanation and with a raised voice said: 'A little problem is it Joey? It's more like a fucking disaster than a little problem Joey! Tell him and the rest of us what's fucking happened?'

Again Joey started to explain what had happened, only this time he left the word *'little'* out of his explanation. I could instantly tell from the way Joey was talking that he knew he was in deep shit with Fred because of the sheepish way he was presenting himself. All eyes were fixed directly on him as he told us what had happened and it wasn't good news from the Firm's point view. Apparently, the Yardies had blatantly fucked Fred's Firm over for £2 million on a cocaine deal. Joey was sweating like a pig as he tried to explain what had gone down, and all the time he was yapping away, Fred was staring at him with a face like thunder. I caught eye contact with a few of the Firm and I could tell from their expressions that they were dying to say 'Told you so.' But, of course, they couldn't say a fucking word because Joey was Fred's son-in-law.

To cut a long story short, the Yardies had sold Joey 100 kilos of novacaine instead of the premium coke they'd promised. When Joey had sussed out what had happened, he decided to try and get the money back before Fred found out. Unfortunately, Joey's plan had not worked out too well because, as I already said, Joey was a fucking psychotic maniac and a liability when it came to dishing out violence. The stupid cunt had no control and no idea of how to do things strategically. He had decided to kidnap one of the Yardie crew he had been doing business with and ended up trying to extort a ransom for him; a sum amounting to what was lost on the coke deal. In his infinite wisdom, he had given the Yardie crew 24 hours to come up with the money or else he would carve up his West Indian captive. The Yardies told Joey to go fuck himself because they did not give a fuck for anyone, even their own. So Joey, true to his word, chopped the fucker up and posted the bits back to them over a seven day period. Joey had thought that by being so ruthless, the Yardies would have second thoughts and return the money. Instead he got the opposite reaction.

When Fred was told of what happened he was thinking of putting out a contract on the leader of the Yardie Firm, and I could only guess that that's why I was there. After Joey had finished his garbled bullshit story, Fred rose from the table and said: 'Well gentleman, has anyone got any ideas on how to deal with this problem?'

My first thoughts were to kill Joey for fucking up and I'm sure it was going through the minds of the others in that room, but Joey was Fred's son in-law, so that option was out of the window. I decided to say fuck-all and let the others come up with an idea; after all, I was bloody retired wasn't I? There were mumbled conversations between them all as they sat at the table. Fred was still standing, fat cigar in his mouth, with his hands on his hips just looking at his crew.

Then one of the geezers at the table, a shrewd bloke called Sammy, addressed Fred with a raised voice so as to be heard over the others: 'Fred! There could be an answer.'

Fred told everyone to keep quiet and let Sammy explain his idea.

'Well if I was you I'd take that contract off the Yardie boss because it will only mean a war, and let's be honest Fred, we can't afford that, can we?'

Fred gestured to Sammy to continue.

'What I suggest is that we set the fuckers up and do to them what they did to us.'

Fred butted in and said: 'How do we go about that then Sammy?'

I could see where Sammy was going with this and he was right to suggest that the contract should be lifted because we definitely could not afford a fucking war. Fred though was very impulsive and wanted results yesterday. Sammy suggested that we set the Yardies up and if we all put our heads together, he was sure we could come up with a plan to get some pay-back.

He was right because there were some really streetwise, intelligent members at that meeting and together they could easily fuck over these Yardies. Their reputation for ruthlessness and violence was well deserved but they were also disorganised and lacked unity. Whilst Sammy was telling us, everyone was nodding their approval except for Joey and me. It was obvious why Joey wasn't agreeing: it would take the situation right out of his hands, making him look like a complete mug with his respect going down the toilet. As I have already said, respect has to be earned and Joey had just lost all of his in one go by doing business with the Jamaicans.

The reason *I* was not agreeing was because I was thinking that this situation could pay huge dividends for me if I used my loaf; and I'm not just referring to money either. Here was a possible way out for me and my wits were working overtime as I weighed up what was going down.

Fred just looked at the ceiling and said: 'What you're suggesting Sammy would take a long time to bear fruit, and you forget I'm two million quid out of pocket. I don't fucking like it! Okay?'

Fred was still standing as he put both hands on the table and leaned over towards the assembled gathering and addressed us all in a very calm, menacing way.

'Gentlemen, take yourselves away and be back here tomorrow with a plan that is not going to take a month of Sundays. Now go and put your thinking heads on and earn the fucking money I pay you all.'

As they all got up from the table I rose as well and was about to leave when Fred said: 'Not you Jack I want a private word with you.'

I sat back down and lit a cigarette while the others made their way through the door. I noticed Joey was still sitting at the other end of the table saying his goodbyes to the boys.

When Fred realised that Joey was still in the room he sarcastically said to Joey: 'What fucking bit of 'I want a private word with Jack' do you not understand Joey?'

Joey just looked at Fred with a supercilious expression then said: 'Oh, okay Fred I get the message, I'll piss off then.'

Fred spoke down to Joey, like a teacher would talk to a naughty pupil and said: 'You won't piss off Joey, you will wait outside this room and no further because I haven't finished with you yet. And while you're waiting, go and make us all a cup of tea okay?'

As he got up, Joey just pushed the chair backwards and it fell back onto an expensive hand carved coffee table with a bang. He was performing like a two year old as he made his way to the door.

Fred waited until Joey's ass was just out of the door when he said loudly: 'Joey!'

Joey stepped back into the room and said: 'Yes Fred?'

'Pick it up.'

Joey took his eyes away from Fred and looked at the chair and before he could move Fred ordered: 'Do it now Joey.'

I could see his face turn a dark shade of purple because of the way Fred was talking to him. He was being humiliated in front of me and spoken to without respect and I could see he was livid. I thought *'I hope he doesn't give Fred any back chat'* because the way Fred's mood was, he would end up with a bullet in the head. Joey bit his lip and reluctantly did as he was told and left the room slamming the door. Fred put his head in his hands as he sat back in his chair and quietly said: 'What the fuck does she see in that useless cunt?'

From what he was saying I gathered he was referring to his daughter. Fred took a deep breath and puffed on his cigar until he had the tip glowing red, and then said to me: 'What do you think about this entire fuck-up Jack?'

I looked at Fred and asked him if I could speak freely.

'Of course you can Jack. Speak as free as you wish; it's your opinion I want, not the way you say it.'

'Well firstly I ain't got a clue why I'm here because you told me I was retired and secondly, if you want my honest opinion, then I think you're a mug for letting that fucking idiot talk you into doing business with those Yardie bastards.'

I waited for his reaction as he just sat there staring at me sucking on that fat Cuban cigar. After a minute or so with us both just staring at each other, Fred said: 'Don't push your luck Jack.'

I answered: 'With respect Fred, you did ask me to tell you how I saw it.'

Fred leaned over the table to get closer to me and said: 'What's our chance of having that Yardie cunt whacked?'

I shook my head as I said to Fred: 'Not good Fred.'

'Why's that?'

'Well, he has just fucked you over for £2 million and he has had one of his foot soldiers posted back to him in pieces. He knows you're not going to leave it there and is probably expecting some more trouble. If I were him I would be on my guard and probably go to ground.'

'So what do we do then?'

My brain was now going ten to the dozen as I tried to come up with a plan that could get me away from this shit while keeping Fred happy at the same time.

'You could always go for second best Fred.'

'What do you mean second best Jack?'

'Well has he got a missus or a kid?'

I got Fred's attention with that question and he said: 'I know where you're coming from son; let's ask silly bollocks outside.'

Fred then roared for Joey to come into the room, and within seconds, he stuck his head around the door and said: 'Yes Fred.'

'Get your ass in here now; I want to ask you something.'

Joey came in and pulled a chair up opposite me and said to Fred: 'Fire away then Fred.'

'Has that Yardie cunt got any family?'

'Joey's reply was near on comical when he replied: 'What do you mean? Like a Mum and Dad?'

Fred got really angry with him and answered as if he was talking to a mug: 'No you dopey cunt, like a wife or kid.'

Joey's eyes lit up and he said: 'Er, I don't know but I can suss what you're getting at.'

Fred was not amused with this idiot.

'Oh you can, can you?'

'Yes Fred, you want to grab them don't you?'

'Listen to me Joey because I'm only going to tell you this once! If I ask you a question then I want an answer, not what you think I'm thinking alright? Now answer the fucking question.'

Joey's face was a picture and, to be honest, I was getting a lot of satisfaction at seeing this jumped up mug being humiliated.

'I don't know, but I can find out for you.'

With that, Fred turned to me and said: 'Now, where were we Jack?'

I was just about to say something when Fred spoke again.

'Joey, what the fuck are you still doing here? Did I ask you stay?'

Joey was now bright red with embarrassment and suppressed rage and got up from the table. He was extra careful this time not to knock another chair over and sheepishly walked out of the room with Fred calling after him for our tea.

'Fred, before you ask, there's no way I'm going to whack a woman or a kid.'

Fred gave me 'the look' and then said: 'You'll do as you're told Jack. Anyway, that's not what I have in mind. Maybe, if he had a missus or kid then we could snatch them.'

I told Fred all I knew about the Yardies, especially about the way the bosses (inasmuch as they have 'bosses') worked. The chances that they would part with £2 million for a kid or wife would be highly unlikely because they were selfish, heartless bastards. I told him that the odds were that he probably had close family safely tucked up back in Jamaica. They never brought immediate family to England because they never stayed in one place for long. From my knowledge, they were mainly illegal immigrants who had overstayed their holiday visas and went underground while they did their business. I also told him that because they never gave a flying fuck about anyone, they never last that long. When their time was up they were either killed by another Yardie, nicked, or wise enough to get back to the West Indies with a fortune and retire.

Fred was all ears and absorbed everything I told him about them.

Finally he said: 'I suppose this cunt has an army looking after him?'

'Too right he has Fred; he can probably do his business without leaving wherever he is holed up.'

I described to him how his men, while they were all making good money, were likely to be committed to him, and in some instances, they would even treat him like a god.

'Fuck me Jack, how the hell do we get close to him or get my money back? Because, after what you have just told me, it looks like there's not much hope.'

'I'm sorry Fred if I'm not telling you what you want to hear, but those are the facts. The rest of the lads knew the score, that's why they suggested to you to leave it and give this piece of work a wide birth.'

Shaking his head he said: 'I should have known better. Instead I let that stupid wanker talk me into it because he said he had everything under control.'

'I'm sorry to have to say this Fred, but Joey knows fuck all about the Yardies, whereas the likes of Sammy and the rest do.'

Fred turned his chair away from me and stared out of the window saying nothing. The silence in the room was disturbed by Joey bringing in the tea tray. As he made his way to the table, I gave Joey a silent gesture to say nothing and leave the room quickly as I took the tray off him. I knew Fred better than most of the lads and with him just sitting there deep in thought, it wouldn't be wise for anyone to approach him, especially Joey. I gently picked up the teapot, poured us both a cup and slid Fred's quietly over to him. He just remained sitting in his chair with his back to me, still thinking.

Chapter Five

Joey's Demise

That night I came home to Hannah with a lot on my mind and presenting that same expression that said *'piss off'* all over my face. Han had sussed that I was thinking about something and left me in my study to get on with it.

Fred had told me to do what the other lads had been instructed to do: think of a plan to get his £2 million back. My thoughts were not fixed on Fred because, to be honest, I didn't give a fuck about his money or his fuck up with the Yardies. My thoughts were strictly focused on using this situation to get me out of the Firm. Han brought me in a drink, sat down in the chair opposite and lit a cigarette. From the way she was looking at me, I knew she was waiting to find out if I was okay.

'You alright Jack?'

I looked up at her pretty face and smiled.

'I'm fine sweetheart; how about you?'

'I'm good.'

I just carried on sitting there in total silence when she said:

'You want to talk about it Jack?'

I looked up at Hannah and replied: 'Talk about what babe?'

'Cut this nonsense Jack and tell me what happened with Fred?'

'What do you want me to tell you?'

'Well you could tell me if you're bloody retired or not because that look on your face says to me that you're back on the payroll. So don't treat me like one of your cronies and talk to me.'

I thought for a moment and decided to tell her that Fred had a little problem and that he just wanted my opinion on it.

She stood up and shouted: 'Fuck you Jack!'

Then she stormed out of the study, slamming the door behind her. I ignored her tantrum and just sat there puffing on my cigarette. Then I had a brainstorm and an idea started to form itself. I quickly stood up stubbed the fag out and grabbed my coat, making my way downstairs.

Han came out from the living room and said: 'Where are you off to now?'

I was in too much of a hurry to answer her as I opened the front door to leave. Hannah came to the door as I left and bawled: 'Jack! Jack! I'm sorry I shouted at you darling.'

Hannah obviously thought I had stormed out after her performance in the study, but that was the last thing on my mind. As I got into my car the tyres made a screech as I drove off fast out of our driveway, making my way over to Camden in North London.

I had come up with an idea which, if done right, could get me out of this forced commitment to Fred without any comeback on me. After an hour of driving through the busy London traffic, I came to a rest and parked up outside the Red Lion pub. This pub was not one of my usual haunts and I knew no one there except one particular geezer called Elroy; a con I had done time with ten years ago. He wasn't like many West Indians in that he spoke with a broad cockney accent. He had also earned respect from the white criminal class and been accepted.

Elroy was a pimp, drug dealer and a thief. To me he was also a sound geezer and a good friend who owed me a favour. Now I was about to cash it in. I knew he had been working out of this boozer from other villains who were not connected to the Firm.

As I walked through the large wooden doors, the place was packed and the noise of people talking to each other was deafening and unintelligible. I noticed that one side of the bar was full of black people and the other side was full of mostly Irish. North London was the location that many of the Irish had settled in after coming over here in the fifties to work on the motorways and in construction. Then, shortly after the Irish settled, the blacks arrived to man London Transport and the two communities lived side by side with no trouble.

I walked into the crowd of black geezers, looking for Elroy. He was six feet five and built like a brick shithouse, so he would stand out in the crowd. He shouldn't have been too hard to find amongst this mob, but I couldn't see him anywhere as I went from one end of the bar to the other. Then someone tugged my jacket and, as I turned to see who had a grip on me, I came face to face with a Rastafarian Bob Marley lookalike.

'Who are you looking for white boy?' he said in his broad Caribbean accent.

I had to smile at this geezer because his hat resembled a tea cosy.

'I'm looking for Elroy mate, do you know him?'

He looked me up and down as he dragged on a big spliff and said: 'Are you friend or Babylon?'

I knew that Babylon meant the Old Bill so I replied: 'Friend.'

Again he looked me up and down as if weighing me up and then said: 'What you want with Elroy?'

Now this tea cosy was getting too nosey and was beginning to irritate me so I said sarcastically: 'Mind your own fucking business *man.*'

The geezer took a step back and eyed me up and down once more and said: 'You're not Babylon man.'

'Well done mate, if you carry on like that you'll win first prize for observation. Now, do you know Elroy or not because I need to see him.'

'Wait here white boy and I will fetch him from his office.'

He then glided off through the crowd and disappeared into a room situated next to the bar. A few moments later, through the smoked filled bar, I got sight of a large-framed geezer coming into view. It was Elroy. The tea cosy pointed over to where I was standing and it was then we made eye contact. The moment Elroy recognised me, his face broke into a wide grin, exposing his pearly white teeth, and he made his way over to me.

'Hello Jack? Long time, no see. What's happening mate?'

I said to Elroy: 'I need a chat with you mate. Is there anywhere we can talk in private?'

'Of course Jack, follow me.'

We made our way through the crowd, heading for his small office.

'After you my friend.'

As we got inside, he locked the door behind him and said: 'It's good to see you Jack. Now I wonder what can I do for you......coke, girls?'

'No coke and no girls Elroy. I just want you to do me a little favour.'

Elroy looked at me with a confident smile and said: 'Is this business Jack?'

'Yeah, you could call it something like that.'

'Okay mate. I'm all ears.'

I gave him a cautious look, as if I was deciding if I wanted to tell him or not. He said: 'Well spit it out then.'

'I need you to make a phone call for me.'

Elroy shook his head, grinned and then said: 'Come off it Jack, you're telling me that you have come all this way to the other side of London to ask me to make a phone call?'

I looked at him straight faced and said: 'Yes mate.'

Elroy's grin began to fade when he realised that I wasn't fucking about.

'You're fucking serious aren't you?'

'You better fucking believe it Elroy because I couldn't be more serious.'

Elroy sat back in his chair and, without taking his eyes off me; he pulled a big spliff from the desk drawer and lit it. He could guess that there was more to my request then just picking up a phone.

'What's in it for me then?'

I hated what he was asking me because I expected him to just say 'yeah and when do you want me to make it Jack?' He knew me well from the old days when we worked together smuggling in heroin from Turkey and cocaine from Brazil. So it was obvious to him that there was a lot more to it than just a phone call.

I answered: 'That favour you owe me will be paid in full Elroy.'

He laughed out loud when I said that.

'Fuck me Jack you've got a memory like a fucking elephant.'

I had to laugh with him and said: 'So you remember then?'

'How could I ever forget Jack, you saved my life…'

I butted in on him before he finished: 'And Rosa's as well'

'Fuck me Jack. You hit below the belt, don't you?'

With the banter now put to one side, I said to Elroy: 'I'm calling in that favour you owe me mate. All's I want from you is to make a call to a certain person and, when you do, I want you to talk in your Rasta accent. That's all; it's not hard work is it Elroy?'

'I take it you're not going to tell me what all this is about then Jack?'

'I can't Elroy. You know the rules mate.'

He just wouldn't leave it there and kept on about how much all this was worth. I was beginning to lose patience with him.

'Elroy please listen to me. This has nothing to do with money, nor am I 'working' on this one. This is all about me not getting my head blown off!'

'Okay Jack, I get the picture; it's not a problem mate. I'll do as you ask with no questions, okay?'

I got up from the chair and gently grabbed him by both ears and jokingly planted a big kiss on his sweaty forehead and said: 'I knew I could rely on you, mate. Now, let me out of this office.'

'Hang on, what about that call you want me to make?'

I smiled at him and said: 'All in good time.'

'Well what do you want me to say?'

'I'll let you know that when I'm ready Elroy, so stop fucking about and open this fucking door before I get stoned off the fumes from that rolled up carpet you're smoking.'

He roared with laughter and patted me on the back as he opened the door and then said: 'I heard you got divorced and that you're now shacked up with a young bird.'

As he walked with me to my car, I told him about Hannah and how she had been ill. His face went near on white when I told him about Junior.

'Fuck me mate, another nipper? You're a sucker for punishment.'

I told him how much I was enjoying myself having Junior around and being part of his life. He listened to me intently as I also explained to him how I nearly ended up as a single parent due to Han's illness.

'I've got respect for you Jack. There's not many like you still about who would take on that responsibility. Not at our age.'

I changed the subject and asked him how Rosa was. Rosa was part of our smuggling team and during that time, she and Elroy had got it together and become an item.

'She got cold feet and packed the game in after those Turks tried to kill the pair of us. She's now married to a builder and has two kids. She's living the straight life up in Peterborough.'

I thought to myself: *'Who could blame her after what she and Elroy went through?'* I had saved their lives after a drug deal went wrong in Rome. I intervened just as the two of them were about to be executed by the Turkish mafia. This was the favour I was now calling in from Elroy.

'I'll be in touch, so don't go on holiday will you?'

Elroy smiled and said: 'It's good seeing you again Jack. I'll wait for your call so take it easy man.'

As I drove away, making my way back to the south side of the river, my thoughts reflected on my conversation with Father Malone and what he had said to me after my confession. I knew he cared about me and that he only wanted the best for me – after all, he was in the business of saving lost souls. It was through him and that little chat we'd had that had given me the resolve to do something about my situation. I often wondered what it would be like to live straight and sin free, and would sometimes watch so-called normal people going about their daily lives. Would I be able to live their way if my plan worked? Would I be satisfied, content and happy? Or was I just kidding myself? Only time would tell.

When I arrived home, it was late and Hannah was still up waiting for me. As I came through the door, we both paused and looked at each other; then she came over to hug me.

'Jack I'm so sorry......'

I raised my finger to her lips to stop her from continuing and said very softly: 'Sshh Han, there's no need for you to say sorry sweetheart; it's me who should be apologising to you.'

I could see from the redness around her eyes that she had been crying and I felt bad for the way she must be feeling. I loved her so much and would have given anything to be able to tell her what I was planning, but, for her own safety, I could not. I gently cupped each side of her face in my hands and tilted her head so she was looking up at me. I kissed her gently on the lips and then said: 'Babe I promise you everything is going to be alright, okay? I need you to stop worrying about me because you know it upsets me to see you like this.'

'Jack you know how much I love you darling. I've never interfered before in your business, but you have been acting so strange recently that I can feel your vibes rubbing off on me. I get this horrible feeling that something bad is going to happen.'

Even though I could see that she was serious, I told her not to be silly.

'But I can Jack, you don't understand how I feel some days, especially with the way you've been so quiet and secretive lately.'

'You know that I can't tell you anything about my work with the Firm. What I can tell you is that I'm doing my best to get things sorted because I promised you I would. Now just trust me to get on with it and stop worrying because everything is going to be hunky dory, okay?'

She looked at me doubtfully, smiled and said: 'My Mother warned me about you Jack, but did I listen?'

I had to laugh at her because her mother had done her best to split the pair of us up when we first got together. My reputation always preceded me wherever I went and she did not want her daughter to be with the likes of me. Unbeknownst to her mum, Hannah had been a bit of a character herself and was one of the best shoplifters I had ever come across. That's how I met her: she came to my mate's house with a load of *Gucci* clothes when I happened to be there. I ended up buying the lot off her. Shortly after that first meeting we started dating and we have been together ever since. It was love at first sight for both of us, but her mum hated it when she found out about me and did her best to put an end to our relationship. But our love for each other was that strong that she had no choice but to accept it, especially when Han fell pregnant with Jack Junior.

Next morning I was up early and, after breakfast, I made my way over to the factory as requested by Fred; only this time I was the first one there. I bumped into Joey as he was coming out of Fred's office.

'Morning Joey, how's Fred?'

Joey's reaction was a mixture of anxiety and fear and he was bouncing around like a frightened kid. I could only assume that Fred had been giving him the third degree, especially after his performance the day before. Joey had always been arrogant and cocksure when the Firm was running smoothly. He would always give the impression that he was a leader of men. Now that the shit had hit the fan, he was like a little boy lost in the woods who couldn't find his way home.

'Find out for yourself Jack; he's in there.'

As I opened the door, I could hear Fred on the phone giving some poor unfortunate a verbal hiding. I made my way to his end of the conference table to take the seat that I'd had the day before. Fred looked up at me and gestured to go to the other end of the table where Joey had been sitting at the meeting yesterday. I'm thinking to myself that poor old Joey had definitely been demoted because that end of the table was always where he sat.

Fred put the phone down, sat back in his chair and said: 'You're early Jack. Has that brat of yours been keeping you up?'

I hated anyone referring to my Jack Junior as a brat because he had a name and Fred knew it. If it had been anyone else, I would have given them a clump, but I had to bite my tongue because it was Fred.

I replied with a tone of slight sarcasm: 'No Fred, Jack Junior hasn't kept me up all night; he's a very sound and contented sleeper.'

My attitude slightly surprised Fred because he wasn't used to people taking that tone with him.

'Well, take a seat Jack and tell me what you've got for me about getting my dough back.'

I broke eye contact with Fred and looked down at the chair.

'But that's Joey's chair Fred.'

Fred slammed the palm of his hand onto the table with a whack.

'Not no more it ain't Jack; now sit and tell me what you've come up with.'

I did as I was told and was now seated facing him. Sitting there gave me a feeling of unwanted power. I had been at this table many times over the years. When I first joined the Firm I was allocated the centre seat because I was not family. Over the years, as my respect grew, I was moved up a seat at a time and eventually ended up being seated next to Fred. Now I was at the opposite end of the table, and I knew when the others turned up, they would automatically think that I had been promoted and back on the Firm.

I said to Fred: 'I hope you're not suggesting that I take over from Joey, Fred?'

'I ain't got fucking time for this Jack. Just do as you're told and sit in the bloody chair. Now, tell me how we are going to get my money back will ya?'

I could see from Fred's behaviour that he was not in the mood to be fucked about so I warily told him: 'I've an idea, but I need a bit of time with it.'

Fred looked angry now and was spitting as he spoke.

'That's the one thing I ain't got Jack, I need something now!'

'Look Fred, if we rush this, then there's more chance it will go tits up and you'll end up with fuck all.'

Just as Fred was going to start ranting and raving, Sammy and the rest of the white collar workers came through the door. As they made their way to their seats, Sammy remained standing and waited for the room to settle.

He hesitated before he spoke to Fred.

'Morning Fred.'

Fred had lit one of his cigars and said his 'good mornings' to him and the boys. Then he focussed his pissed off expression on Sammy.

'Well Sammy I hope you've had better luck than Jack. He's telling me that he needs more time to come up with something.'

'I'm sorry to say Fred that Jack's right. We *do* need more time. We could fuck it up if we rush head on into it and you're not going to like that. Just be patient Fred and let me explain…'

Fred brusquely interrupted Sammy as the poor sod was trying to reason with him and shouted: 'Don't you, or anyone of you, tell me to be fucking patient. When I ask for results, I want fucking results! Now all of you can sit in this room until you come up with a viable working plan that's not going to take time. Do I make myself clear gentlemen?'

We all nodded in compliance. Then, out of the blue, Fred burst past us leaving a trail of smoke in his wake, as he left the office, slamming the heavy door behind him and shouting Joey's name. I smiled as I thought of poor old Joey about to get it in the neck again. After all, it was his entire fault that Fred was in this mess.

Everyone in the room sighed with relief once we heard Fred's car start and drive away. Sammy looked at me and remarked on me sitting in Joey's chair.

'What's this then Jack? Since when have you been family?'

I stopped Sammy in his tracks and got up from the chair and went to my usual seat; then spoke to them all.

'Listen to me you lot, I'm not family and never will be. This chair business was Fred's idea because he's pissed off with Joey, so cut the snide remarks.'

One of the geezers at the table was a bloke called Benny who was in charge of the casinos and betting offices that the Firm had controlled. He took charge of the situation because he could see that I was getting angry.

'Slow down Jack and take it easy! Let's all stay calm and work this shit out.'

I could see that everyone was getting stressed and the last thing the situation needed, was me kicking off at Sammy. Besides, creating a volatile state of affairs was not part of my plan. Benny told Sammy to leave it out with the snide remarks and concentrate on the job in hand. Then he coolly spoke to everyone.

'Lads please, there's no reason to treat Jack differently from the rest of us. He's been around this Firm a lot longer than most of you, so he's as good as family.'

He leaned forward in his chair and put his hand out to me. We both shook hands and I acknowledged a nod of his head as an apology. He then asked us all to get down to business.

I decided to stay quiet and let them get on with it. Sammy started waffling on about doing a drugs deal whereby they could hijack the drug shipment. Benny brought up a significant point.

'There's a slight problem with your idea Sammy. How on earth do we get this Yardie crew to do business with us again without them sussing that it's a setup?

I butted in and told them: 'Let's face it lads, you're wasting your time dreaming up another drug deal with those animals. Your best bet would be to go after the bastard who has Fred's money. You don't stand a chance in conning the fuckers. They're so slippery that they would be expecting a comeback. Apart from that, how the fuck do you expect to do it in record time?'

Benny agreed with me while Sammy was sitting with his head in his hands.

I made a point of reminding them that Fred was putting them all under a lot of pressure. And from my experience, any crew that worked like that would most definitely bollocks things up.

Another family member called Mike asked: 'Well, what are we going to do then? Fred isn't going to be too happy if we don't come up with something soon.'

Again I spoke out to remind them that they were limited with their options. Joey had simply caused more trouble and made the problem worse by cutting up one of the Yardie crew and posting him back in pieces. He thought that would be enough to scare the pants off them and get Fred's money back. But the only response Joey got was to be told to go and fuck himself. Sammy had a change of mind from the day before because now he wanted to go to war with the fuckers. Benny and the rest were quite right to object to his idea because that wouldn't get Fred his £2 million back.

I got up from the table and said to them all: 'I'm off home lads because, as far as I can see, you lot are getting nowhere with this.'

Sammy mentioned to me that Fred wouldn't be too happy with me if I upped and left before they sorted something out.

I said to him: 'Well if that's the case, tell Fred I'll pop round to his house tonight; then I can explain myself to him directly.'

Benny was surprised with my lax attitude and asked me if I was sure I wanted to do that.

'Of course I'm sure Benny, just make sure to pass the message on for me okay?'

I left them to get on with it and made my way to my car smiling. What had just happened was now the start of my newly formed plan. I knew they couldn't come up with anything at such short notice. Fred knew that as well. That's why he wanted me there, hoping that, with my input, they might come up with a result.

Chapter Six

'The Setup'

After the meeting with the Firm I needed time to be on my own to work out what was next on my agenda. I thought over what had been said by the lads and I was confident enough to know they wouldn't be able to come up with anything that would keep Fred happy. Early that evening, I decided to go and see Fred and face the music.

As I was pulling in to Fred's driveway, I noticed his Roller parked up with the offside caved in badly. I thought to myself that he's really going to kick off now because that car was his pride and joy. A quick thought did go through my head that the driver of the other car that was involved must now be quite popular with a few hit-men. Knowing Fred as I did, I wouldn't have put it past him to have the driver whacked.

Fred opened the door with a face like thunder before I could ring the bell. He gripped me by the coat and pulled me inside the door and into his study then said 'Have I got '**MUG**' tattooed on my forehead?'

My thoughts were right. Fred was foaming at the mouth and pacing all over his study like a man possessed.

'Well Jack?'

I said almost humbly: 'No Fred, I don't think you've got a sign on your head saying ***MUG***.'

He was panting heavily now and started taking deep breaths to control his breathing. I just stood there in silence waiting for the rest of his onslaught. After a minute he had regained his composure and said: 'Then what bit of *'stay here and sort my problem out'* didn't you understand?'

I straightened up my posture and looked Fred square in the eyes and replied: 'Look Fred those boys were not getting anywhere and, if I'm honest, they couldn't sort a piss-up in a brewery.'

Fred let rip on me and his arm was now outstretched with his finger pointing at me.

'So you thought you could just walk out Jack?'

'No Fred, I thought that I would come and see you later, so I could put an idea to you without the others being around.'

Fred's eyes lit up and he lowered his arm and spoke calmly.

'Why, have you got a way of sorting this bit of business out then Jack?'

I had to be very careful how I was going to answer that question because Fred would take my answer as gospel.

'I do have an idea Fred and I think it's the best one you're going to get considering how badly Joey fucked things up for you.'

Fred changed back into Mr Angry when Joey's name was mentioned and started raising his voice, so I knew what I was saying to him was having the desired effect.

He roared: 'That fucking Joey is a walking liability Jack. If it wasn't for my daughter's sake I'd invite the fucker for lunch at my pig farm.'

Fred was doing everything I anticipated and Joey was now a key component in my plan.

'Well Jack. Tell me what I want to hear?'

I paused for a moment to regain composure after which I said to him: 'I've got access to one of the Yardie crew and he is willing to do business. For the right price he is willing to pass shit hot information over to us.'

'What sort of info?'

I smiled at Fred and said: 'The sort of info that tells us when and where their next coke shipment is arriving and who the buyer is. Also, Fred he is willing to tell you where you can find the Yardie boss.'

On Fred's face was a look that contained a mixture of relief with an inkling of suspicion. He told me to continue and started to pace slowly around his study looking at the carpet and cupping his chin with his hand. I stood there just looking at this feared crime boss pondering over what I had just told him. I was taking an almighty risk trying to work Fred because he was a very clever man under all that swagger and anger. He even had a degree in psychology, which he picked up while doing a ten stretch at HMP Durham back in the seventies. Having that made him a qualified people reader, and a clever one with it.

'That's a tasty bit of information you've come across there Jack,' Fred said as he continued to walk slowly around the study.

'I know it is Fred. In fact, it's solid gold mate.'

'Then why didn't you come out with this at the meeting?'

'I couldn't because my source is known to one of the Firm and they don't exactly get on.'

'Who's the grass Jack?'

'He's a mate of a geezer I done a bit of bird with years ago.'

'So why is this Yardie willing to grass on his own; what's his motive Jack?'

This was where I couldn't fuck up because Fred was now slowly interrogating me so as to satisfy himself with what I was offering.

'Joey killed and cut up his brother Fred and he wasn't too happy about that. Then he became pretty pissed off that his boss never did fuck-all about it apart from line his own pockets. To add insult to injury, his boss never even financially sorted his brother's family out either. So I reckon his motive is quite feasible and genuine Fred.'

Fred stopped pacing and told me to sit down and offered me a drink. I knew at that moment I had passed his test because the atmosphere was now lighter and boy, did I need that drink?'

Fred sat down at his desk cupping a large brandy with both hands watching the drink as he swirled it around gently.

'So what does he want?'

'Well Fred you might not like what I'm about to say. I'm only telling you what he told me, so don't do your nut okay?'

Fred looked up from his glass and said: 'I'll be the judge of that.'

I took a deep breath and carried on.

'He wants Joey whacked plus two hundred grand up front. For that, he's willing to give us everything we need.'

I wasn't expecting what came next because he had taken what I had just told him too calmly. Fred was slowly nodding his head but he stayed surprisingly silent; just staring at his drink. I had been expecting him to explode when I told him about Joey but he didn't really show any emotion. Fred then raised his head to make eye contact with me and put the glass down on the table with a bit of a thump, spilling some of the contents.

'How does he expect me to whack my son-in-law? And how do we know that his info is on the level? And another thing, what makes you think that this Yardie bastard isn't working you Jack?'

I confidently answered his questions.

'As I have already said Fred, he's a mate and a sound geezer who I can assure you is on the level. He's mighty pissed off with Joey because of what he did to his brother, and his boss for not doing fuck all. He now knows he can't carry on working for his posse because there's no respect anymore, and has decided he wants out. He also wants pay-back and told me to tell you *'It's only business with his boss, but it's personal with Joey.'* The request for Joey comes from the dead geezer's family Fred. They believe in a life for a life. He also knows that he can't come back at Joey because of the Firm, so he's left the ball in your court.'

Fred said: 'Find out what he's got Jack and get back to me okay? And for his sake, it'd better be bloody good if he wants to keep on breathing. That's a fucking tall order he's asking for. However, you've given me something to think about and that's more than I can say for the others. Keep this quiet Jack and don't make him any promises without my say-so, okay?

'Will do Fred.' I said with relief.

Fred stood up to direct me out of his study and said: 'I want something done fast Jack, don't you forget that son.'

'I do understand and I'll do my best, but I can't promise you because it is out of my hands. I think the way the Yardie is setting this up is that he's put it down to you on how long this work is going to take mate.'

'Don't you think I know that? Listen Jack, do your best and get everything out of this fucker okay?'

As I left his office and got into my car, I could feel the sweat running down my back into the crack of my ass cheeks. I sat in the car with the window open and took a lung full of fresh air. It felt good knowing that my plan was beginning to take shape. I also knew not to count my chickens before they had hatched or get over-confident because working Fred was not an easy task. He had amazing ways about him that baffled the best of those who had done business with him. He could be totally unpredictable and had a confusing habit of suddenly changing his mind.

I made my way back home to Hannah and Junior. It was such a nice feeling knowing that they were waiting for me. Only at home could I climb out of the invisible suit of armour that I wore every time I went out. Within my four walls I could be the person I wanted to be: a loving caring man who treasured his Hannah and Jack Junior. I never socialised with the boys on the Firm. I hated mixing business with pleasure because I would have had to keep up the pretence of gangsterdom. I liked being myself with my family, especially being a Dad and a loving partner. Hannah would always say to me that I was a big softie underneath that armour of mine. She would often take the piss by threatening me that she would tell the rest of the Firm what I was really like. I had always kept my private life separate from them; that way I could switch off when I got home. I now realised that Father Malone knew that there was more to me than just a gangster and a cold blooded killer. He could suss that there was compassion within me and he especially, knew that I wanted out of the grips of Fred and the Firm.

'Hello babe, there's a salad in the fridge. I didn't know what time you were getting back so I didn't want to cook something and have it ruined.'

I just smiled at Hannah because she was the perfect woman: not too many questions and very considerate.

'Thanks sweetheart I'll have a quick shower then eat after. How's Junior babe?

'He's fine, just a bit humpy that's all.'

'A bit like you then Han,' I said, teasing.

She warned me not to take the piss or she would come over and knock me out. I had to laugh at her sometimes because she could act like a geezer with all the masculine mannerisms to go with it. She could also be very feminine and sexy when we were being romantic; to me she was the ideal woman. I would pity any burglar that came across my Han if she caught them robbing our house; she was one fearless girl who could handle herself. Fourth Dan karate, black belt judo and a dab hand with her nunchucks was my Hannah and I loved her like no other woman I had ever met.

After I ate and Junior was all tucked up for the night, Han came over and sat with me on the sofa. She smiled and softly said: 'You look a lot less stressed sweetheart, are things working out for you?'

I gave her a knowing look followed by a smile and replied: 'Don't give up do you babe?'

Han giggled and said: 'Just nice to see you a bit happier Jack that's all.'

'Yeah, alright babe and I'm a vicar.'

I knew she was dying to know if I was still on track with my plan and she was just buttering me up to get me talking. When she worked me this way, I had a tendency to give in to her because her allure could be awesome, especially if we ended up between the sheets. In a way, it was a form of foreplay with a game that had a touch of fantasy attached to it.

'We're doing fine Han, my plan is working better than I first thought and it's 'all systems go.' I said jokingly.

She jumped right on to my lap all excited and begged me to tell her more. This was the second stage of our foreplay and I knew where we were heading.

'Sorry M'am, I am unable to divulge confidential information and I suspect that you are now going to torture me to gain access to my top secret knowledge.'

She gave me a breathtakingly sexy look and whispered in my ear: 'I sure am sunshine and did you know that '*Ve have vays of making you talk*'?'

Excitedly I played along.

'P23908657 Captain Jack Smith, that's all you're getting from me.'

Han was now getting turned on big time. She was sitting astride me knicker-less and I could see her sweet juices were running down her silky thighs dripping on to my lap. She leaned forward to put her lips to my ear and whispered in a real sexy, horny voice: 'We have a new weapon Captain Smith..... Which can suck all that top secret information out of you.'

'You can try your secret weapon but I assure you madam that I am a professional soldier and trained in torture techniques so there is nothing that you can do to me that will make me talk.'

'You want a bet Captain Jack?'

'Han dropped to her knees and undid my trousers, pulling them half way down. Taking my now throbbing cock in her left hand and cupping my balls with her right hand, she raised her face to look at me with her gorgeous eyes. Gazing up at me she took the tip of my cock into her sweet mouth and licked the underside of my bell end gently with her pretty pink tongue. Just that look from those beautiful eyes made me explode into her mouth. I shook uncontrollably as I unloaded my cum. She gestured for me to look down, then she showed me the contents of her sweet mouth, swirling my spunk from side to side with her tongue. Then she swallowed. She gently squeezed every drop from me and continued to suck and caress my dick until the blood flow decreased and left it slippery from her saliva. As I gazed down, I watched her wash the full length of my cock by deep-throating me, taking it in right up to the hilt.

'I give up, I'll tell you everything; that secret weapon of yours is too powerful for me.' I said play-acting.

We both just looked at each other then pissed ourselves laughing at our little show. It felt so good to laugh because it seemed so long since we had. We spent the next two hours making love like teenagers. We must have shagged in every room in the house. We ended our love session on the washing machine. I would lift Han up and sit her on the top, spreading her legs wide. I would enter into her soaking tight wet pussy and take hold of her cute tiny waist with my huge hands and switch the machine onto full spin. All we had to do was to hang on to each other and let the washing machine do its business until we both came. It gave the words '*fully automatic*' a whole new meaning.

So I recommend the washing machine method. Perhaps they should add that to the Karma Sutra.

Chapter Seven

'Fred's Decision'

It was now time to get back in touch with Elroy. Only this time I needed to talk to him about doing a bit more than just making a phone call. What I had in mind for Elroy could change his whole life, especially if it went wrong, so I would have to be very careful how I presented it to him. I needed him even more now because he had now become the most important part of the jigsaw. He had to agree to do the extra work otherwise my plan would be a non-starter. I also had to be straight with him and tell him what the score was and hope he didn't say no. If he did, what would I do? Trust him and hope he doesn't say a word? It would take a lot of trust to do that. The safest way would be to whack him if he rejected my plan and treat it as business. But I also had respect for him. After all, he was a good friend and we had known each other a long time. Would it be fair for me to play with his life?

My plan was devised to get me out and away from the likes of Fred and Joey. That pair of bastards had total control over my life, (even though I was supposed to be retired) and I hated it. I thought about Fred, who was in a similar situation. He had to make a decision on whether his son-in-law lived or died. I knew deep down that I trusted no one which meant that I would have to go through with it if Elroy said no. I was justifying my thinking with thoughts of Hannah and Junior because I was doing all of this for them? Were they not the most important thing in my life today? Too right they were, they were precious to me and I only wanted the best of what life had to offer. They certainly wouldn't have life's treasure while I was still tied to Fred, so my mind was now made up. I had made a decision that I would meet Elroy in a safe place and be tooled up just in case…

Hannah and I went out that night for a quiet meal without Junior. We had arranged for Hannah's mother to babysit him overnight, giving us some well-earned quality time together. We often went to this nice little restaurant well out of the manor in Sidcup. It served up excellent traditional English food and we had used it ever since we got together. My reputation hadn't spread that far so we were treated just like normal people. If we ate locally, we always had kiss ass waiters and managers around us. They would ask us pathetic questions on whether the food was up to par or could we pass their respects on to Fred and Joey. It was all patronising bullshit; for all we knew they could have been out the back playing with our food. So this place was our favourite; no fuss and no bullshit and good food.

As we tucked in, I asked Hannah where she would like to settle.

Her reaction was comical: ‘Are you being serious Jack?’

‘What do you mean am I being serious?’ I said smiling.

‘You know what I mean. I knew there was more to this night out than meets the eye, so stop messing me about.’

I had to laugh at Han because I could see that she was getting annoyed She hated it when I stayed quiet. It would wind her up, and the more I did it, the more she would get pissed off. She had no patience and seeing her do her nut was priceless and had me in stitches. I had to be careful that I didn’t go too far though because Hannah had a wicked temper if pushed over the limit.

‘Okay then Han, it’s time to start making plans about where we are going to end up.’

‘Will we have to look over our shoulders Jack?’

I had to think before answering her.

‘Not if everything goes to plan babe.’

‘Oh Jack, does this really mean that we will be free from the Firm?’

I looked at her sweet face and could see the expression of relief and joy as I told her: ‘Yes babe, completely free and no more of being at their beck and call’

‘How are we going to live? What are we going to do for money?’

‘Calm down Han, the money side is part of my plan and, if all goes well, then we will end up with a nice few quid?’

‘You know what I’m like Jack; I get a bit dizzy sometimes and I know I shouldn’t ask, but please, please tell me more sweetheart.’

I said jokily: ‘Don’t push your luck babe.’

She looked at me with her pitiable expression. If I hadn’t known her, I would have given her the shirt off my back because she was that convincing. I didn’t want to tell her too much but that look had me and I decided to tell her a little bit more.

‘What I can tell you is this. When this bit of work goes down babe, we can’t just disappear. We have to stay and front it out because there are going to be a lot of questions and finger-pointing.’

She butted in on me, saying: ‘You’re the best Jack when it comes to that, I should know, shouldn’t I? I’ve seen you pull some amazing strokes that others would never believe, so I’m not worried there.’

‘The reason I asked you where you wanted to settle Han is because, if it does go pear shaped, then we've got to be prepared and have a safe place to go to.'

'Didn't you say that you could sort Junior out with a first class education in Goa Jack?'

She was spot on with that because for ten pounds a day I could hire a university professor to teach my boy.

'What made you think of India Hannah? I thought you would have wanted northern Cyprus or Spain.'

'Because, from what you've told me, you seemed to know the place pretty well. You've even had the police commissioner on the take and, apart from that, you've always spoken of the place with such passion. Plus, it's bloody hot.'

Han was right. Goa for me, was a place where I could be myself and hang the armour up once and for all. I had been going there for many years before I met Hannah. I loved the place so much that my dream was to retire and live the easy life out there.

'Okay babe it's Goa then.'

Hannah couldn't contain her excitement any longer and quickly got up to give me a hug, taking the table cloth with her. I ended up with my half-eaten meal in my lap along with our drinks. There are not many things that embarrass me, but a big wet greasy stain on my crutch area did, especially when my car was parked up half a mile away. We decided to call it a night and left, making our apologies for Hannah's little mishap. It was good to see her so happy considering what she had been through.

The following morning I was up at dawn and taking a bit of 'me time'. I had learnt later in life to make the most of this time of day. I met a wise old Guru out in India who taught me the art of meditation. Surprisingly, I adopted the art very easily and found that it helped me to keep focussed throughout my day. It was six-thirty when I was interrupted by the phone ringing. My first thought was: 'it's Fred', but I was surprised to hear Sammy's voice.

'Before you tell me to fuck off Jack, I need to have a private word with you.'

'Morning Sammy. Where and what time?' I said in a cheerful, happy voice.

Sammy's reply was laughable.

'Fuck me Jack; you ain't been up all night on the Charlie, have you mate?'

I had to laugh at his comment and replied: 'You've never rung me at this time in the morning before have you Sammy?'

'No Jack, I thought you would have been dead to the world at this time. So, why are you up at the crack of dawn; is it your nipper?'

His remark pissed me off and I said to him:

'What is it with you lot that you keep asking me if my nipper is keeping me up all night? How many more times do I have to tell you? He sleeps like a log and never keeps me up. I'm always up at this time mate. In fact, I've been up an hour already.'

Sammy laughed then made a wisecrack.

'You shit the bed then Jack?'

'Don't push your luck Sammy. Now, where and when?'

We agreed to meet later that day at a second-hand car lot over in Camberwell that was used as a front business for the Firm. I could half guess what Sammy wanted, but instead of trying to project, I left it at the back of my mind. Now was the time to ring Elroy and get my plan operational.

'Please leave a message after the tone' was what I got from Elroy's answering machine. I never, ever left messages on those things, and especially not Elroy's, because it could get me into serious trouble if I had to put a bullet into him later. I've seen people get a lot of jail time for making that kind of stupid mistake while tracking down their intended victim. Hence, it was wise to say fuck all to those machines and always use a public phone box.

It was obvious that Elroy wouldn't surface till the afternoon so I decided to meet up with Sammy first, then move on to him later. In the meantime, I went back home to put my gun away because I did not want to carry that around with me while I was meeting with Sammy.

'Hello babe, you back already?' Hannah said to me as she greeted me with Junior in her arms.

'I've got a few hours to kill before I'm due out again, so I thought I might have a bit of quality time with you sweetheart.'

'You'll be lucky Jack. I have to get Junior down the doctors for his jabs.'

I smiled and said: 'Wishful thinking Han. It's good for me you know.'

She wasn't in the mood for anything and said: 'You can put the kettle on for me sweetheart and make me a cuppa while I get your son washed and dressed,'

That took the romance right out of the situation.

I made my way to the car-lot to meet Sammy. As I said earlier, I had a good idea why he wanted a chat with me. On arriving, I parked my motor up around the corner and made my way on foot through the rear and entered the office.

Startled, Sammy gasped: 'Fuck me Jack! You scared the life out of me mate. I wish you wouldn't creep up on me like that. Don't you know I've got a dodgy ticker?'

I laughed at Sammy's reaction because he had a heart as healthy as a race horse, but he was deaf as a post and could basically hear fuck all.

'Stop whining you old cunt and tell me what you want?'

'Right' he said, 'I've had a word with Fred and he tells me that there is a plan in progress; I just wanted you to know that.'

What he was telling me was music to my ears because it was obvious he never had a clue that I was behind the plan. That meant that Fred had not mentioned my name and kept me out of it. I also suspected Sammy was fishing to find out if I knew more than him.

'What happened then Sam, did you lot come up with something?'

Sammy smiled and said: 'No such luck Jack. After you went, we ended up rowing between ourselves and never got no further.'

'Well who did then?'

'We thought it might have been you Jack, seeing that you were popping into Fred's that night.'

Straight faced, I replied: 'No mate, you got that wrong. All's I got was a bollocking from Fred.'

I could see that Sammy was pondering over our conversation so I decided to keep him busy.

'Did you see the state of his Roller?'

It worked like a dream because Sammy was full of it once I mentioned the car.

'Fucking right I did Jack. His missus took it out and side clumped it at Tesco's.'

We both stared at each other for a second or two then we both burst out in laughter at the same time.

After the laughter died down, I decided to pump Sammy for all he knew.

'Well Sammy, do you know what's happening then?'

'Jack I went round to Joey's and it was him that told me that something was up.'

I weighed up what Sammy was saying, then went a bit further.

'How about Fred, did you go and see him?'

'Yeah, went there after you had left but he never let on. So, I'm none the wiser. He just told me to tell the others that things were going to be sorted out, that's why I belled you.'

'What, at that time in the morning?' I said in disbelief.

'Well, to be honest Jack, I had been up all night trying to think of what Fred was up to. You know me, I'm a worrier.'

He was right there; Sammy always was the sort to worry, especially where Fred was concerned.

'So what do we do now?'

Sammy just looked at me, then winked and said: 'Wait Jack. Just wait and see what the mad cunt comes up with.'

I made a bit of small talk with him, then made my excuses and left. I got to my motor; then decided to call Elroy.

'Hello Jack, good to hear from you man.'

'Hello mate, so you're out of your pit then?'

'Yeah man, had a late one last night.'

'Fucks sake Elroy, talk fucking English will ya?'

'Sorry Jack, been around the brother's all night.'

'We need to meet buddy, but not over your side of the river. Can you meet me at the boozer we use to hang out at in Abbey Wood?'

'Yeah, but it will take me a bit of time to get there. I've got a few loose ends to sort out today. How about seven tonight, that okay with you?'

'No worries mate. Seven it is and don't be late.' I said in a pleasant tone. After all, I didn't want to sound too serious, otherwise I might scare him off. Elroy knew I had put a few people in the ground, especially when I got him and Rosa out of the shit. That day I think I killed two geezers. I say *think* because I didn't hang around after the bullets went flying. So Elroy knew I could be a dangerous man and not to be fucked about with. He also knew I had the edge on him because of that incident with the Turkish mafia. He owed me big time.

I got home to find the house empty which was lucky because it gave me a chance to collect my thoughts and sort my clothes out. On any piece of work I would always wear clothes that I could afford to burn. Hannah would have had her suspicions if she saw me sorting through my work clothes. That would start her worrying and that's the last thing I wanted. I went into my garage where my car was. I opened the boot and cleared everything out and vacuumed the whole area. I then placed sheets of plastic in the boot. This was necessary preparation in case I had to whack Elroy. The reason I wanted our meet in Abbey Wood was because it was nice and quiet and out of the way. Nearby was a large school with coal fed boilers and no live-in caretaker. I had used that boiler to dispose of a target a few months earlier. Being coal fed meant it could be used as a furnace; hot enough to turn bone into powder. This would be Elroy's final resting place if things went wrong. I was praying that he would go along with my plan and I was prepared to give him a nice earner if he agreed. I just hoped he saw it the same way as me.

The gun I was to take with me would be a .38 Smith and Wesson with a silencer. The bullets would be dumb-dumb which meant the tips had been filed down leaving a flat-shape tip. This type of bullet does incredible damage. It's a very quick and painless way to die, but can be messy and the last thing I wanted was to make Elroy suffer. I at least owed him the decency of a quick and painless death if his answer was no.

I had managed to get everything ready before Han came back with Jack Junior. I even cooked a shepherd's pie and laid the table, as well as having a quick clean-up around the house. Hannah came through the door with Junior screaming his head off.

'What's up with him then?'

As she put him into his cot she gave me a funny look and said:' I worry about you sometimes Jack.'

'Whys that then Han, can't I be worried about my kid without you being sarcastic?'

'Jack, he has just been used as a pincushion babe. Don't you remember me telling you this morning that I was taking him to the doctor's?'

'Sorry sweetheart, I've had a bit of a busy day and forgot about the appointment.'

The boy had stopped crying and Hannah stood up right next to the cot with her hands on her hips.

'Too busy my ass, Jack.'

I gave her a confused look and then she let loose.

'Jack the house looks spotless, I can smell cooking so it's obvious that you're up to something.'

'Listen Hannah, sometimes it's like living with a fucking Old Bill with you. I can't take a crap without you asking if I'm up to something. Just because I cooked a bit of grub and cleaned the fucking house doesn't mean that I'm up to something. Anyway, have you forgotten Han? I'm a fucking villain and I'm always up to something so think! Before you start on me again okay?'

Hannah started to sob.

'I'm sorry Jack I didn't mean to get on your back. I know you have a lot on and it was unfair of me to have a go at you. It's just that recently, things are getting a bit too much for me and I'm getting ratty. I'm sorry.'

I just looked at her sweet face and gestured her to come towards me and, once she was in reach, I put both hands out to her. She clasped both my palms, moved in close and we kissed. I gave her a cuddle and whispered in her ear: 'Everything is going to be alright babe. I love you with all my heart and only want the best for you and Junior. Have trust in me sweetheart and let me get on with what it is I'm doing; with no questions asked, okay?'

She looked up at me and said: 'Can I just ask you one teeny weensy question darling?'

Looking down upon that innocent face she was putting on, how could I refuse?

'When will all this be over Jack?'

I paused and answered her: 'Maybe a week but more like two. It depends on what happens when the shit hits the fan.'

'So are we playing it by ear then?'

'That's two questions Hannah.'

She laughed as she wiped her eyes and then asked what was cooking.

'Only the best Han – shepherd's pie.'

'That's nice, do you want me to take over and dish it up?'

She seemed to be more relaxed and contented since our little chat and that was good to see.

As I drove over to Abbey Wood that evening, I was feeling anxious about my meet with Elroy. I kept looking in the rear view mirror at my reflection. I wanted to see if my facial expression was showing signs that I was up to something. In any situation like the one I was about to go into, it was important that I had my poker face on: a facial expression that no-one could read. It was much easier to pull off with people I didn't know, but I had to be on my toes with Elroy because he knew me well and had seen me in all types of situations, especially work mode. So it was fair to say, he was going to be a tough nut to crack.

I parked my car a few streets away from the boozer. I had my gun tucked into the rear of my trousers which I covered with a long Crombie overcoat. It was ten to seven when I entered the saloon bar area. I was a bit early, which gave me time to settle into work mode. The pub was quiet and had a look that suggested it hadn't been decorated since the 'thirties, with paint peeling off the walls and high ceilings. There were only a few old boys drinking up at the bar and no one paid attention to me as I ordered two beers. I found a nice little table with seats in an alcove out of sight of the bar. There was a mirror hanging opposite and in its reflection I had a good view of the pub door.

Dead on seven Elroy came through the door. Immediately, the few that were up at the bar turned to look at this black giant coming into their pub. I leaned forward in my seat and turned my head in the direction of Elroy. He noticed me immediately and grinned, showing off those pearly whites as he strode towards me. I stood up to greet him and gestured to him to take the beer which was in front of him.

'This fucking place hasn't changed has it?'

I looked around the place and agreed with him, then pointed to a big black stain on the worn carpet.

'Remember that Elroy?'

'Remember what Jack?' he said as he looked at the area I was pointing at.

'That! The fucking bloodstain. Don't you remember it?'

Elroy looked puzzled as he took a sip of his beer.

'You've lost me.'

'Do you remember that night when Danny Harris got shot?'

I got his attention with that and he said: 'Fuck me Jack, are you telling me that stain is Danny's blood?'

'Fucking right I am. The tight bastards couldn't even be bothered to put another carpet down; it's fucking disrespectful'

Elroy said: 'It's typical of this pub. Always been a shit hole.'

We both sat there taking deep gulps of our beer until we put our glasses down at precisely the same time.

'Well Jack, what's happening?'

I paused for a moment and quickly thought to myself *'I hope he goes for this.'*

'How would you like to earn yourself £40,000 Elroy?'

He stopped midway through picking up his drink; he was motionless as if frozen in time. Then he answered me.

'What for; a fucking phone call?'

He knew I was up to something when I said: 'There's a bit more to it now than a phone call Elroy. Not much, but a bit more.'

'What does 'a bit more' mean?'

I was about to speak when he butted in.

'Spit it out Jack instead of going all around the houses.'

'Okay mate, I'll get to the point. I want you to phone someone for me pretending to be a Yardie. You'll then work to a script that I will give to you. A few days later, I want you to drive into a car park at night dressed as a Rasta and get out of the car and just stand there. Are you getting what I'm saying mate?'

'Yeah, but I'm waiting for the catch.'

At that moment I decided to go shit or bust with Elroy because he was no mug and he deserved respect.

'Okay Elroy. I'm going to kill Fred and Joey and I'm going to do it in the car park where you will be. To get the pair of them there, I have had to come up with a ploy and your part of it. I can tell you that you won't have to do fuck all. It's easy money and no one knows, except me, that you're involved. There would be no chance of anyone recognising you because you'll be dressed as Bob Marley lookalike. So, what do you say Elroy?'

I then sat back into the chair and took a deep breath. As I put my half empty glass to my lips, I kept my eyes on his. The situation resembled a psychic mind game. He just stared at me with his mouth half open and then leaned over towards me and whispered: 'Are you serious Jack?'

I nodded a yes and watched him as he broke eye contact with me and looked at the floor. It was his way of thinking through what I had just proposed. I broke the silence by standing up and asked him if he wanted another drink.

'Make mine a large brandy.'

While I was at the bar waiting for our drinks I looked at the huge mirror that was behind the jump. I could see Elroy in its reflection sitting side on to me as I watched him intently. He was leaning over with his forearms resting on his huge thighs as he sat forward on his stool. He kept rubbing his hands onto his trousers; probably because his palms were sweating. I knew his brain was going into overdrive, but if the truth be known, so was mine. It would only need him to give me a knock back and my plan would be fucked.

I came back to the table with two large brandies (I was in need of one myself by now.) He hastily took his out of my hand and, with one gulp, emptied his glass. I sat back down and jokily remarked on his drinking.

'That stuff will fucking kill you if you drink it like that mate.'

'Jack, I need to know why mate? You have to put me in the picture because what you're asking me to do could be fucking suicide for the two of us if it went wrong.'

I had already made up my mind to tell him everything because you can't give a geezer like Elroy limited information. There was the risk that he might ask for more money. If, for instance he got nicked, he would be on a murder charge, even if he didn't pull the trigger. As I said, he owed me big time and I was calling that in; as well as giving him £40,000.

'Okay Elroy. I have been trying to get out of the Firm since Hannah got ill. But instead of letting me retire, that pair of cunts have got me whacking people. The last hit I had to do was a fucking nonce Elroy. I know we all say that we could mangle those worthless maggots to bits if given the chance. But those two had me torturing that piece of shit for a long time.'

I went on to tell him about what the women had done, then me having to cut him up and feed him to the pigs.

'Fuck me Jack you actually done that?'

'I had to mate. That's what I mean; they've got me at their beck and call. It wasn't too long ago I was pushing a heavy duty screw driver into some geezer's brain. When I started this, I thought I would only have to whack a few a year. You know, the traditional way: a treble tap with a .45. But these fuckers want me to act out like a fucking animal.'

'I bet it was Joey's idea to get you doing that shit.'

I was starting to feel angry when I said: 'It's his fucking bright idea to big himself up to the local Firms. He thinks that word will get out that our Firm dishes out the harshest punishments and that way he'll earn respect on a par with Fred. But the truth is, he's thick as shit and a psychotic lunatic.

'I heard he was getting a bit of a reputation because he's pissed off lots of people. The truth is, he will never be able to get on a par with Fred.'

'Fred feels the same mate.'

'What do you mean Jack?'

'The only reason the prick is still breathing is because he's Fred's son-in-law.'

I then told him all about Joey and the Yardie incident along with Fred's £2 million going missing. Elroy's ears pricked up when he heard about the cash, but quickly realised he had no chance of getting his hands on it when I explained where it had landed up. We started to settle with each other and our understanding was beginning to take shape. The nervousness for us both was now slowly dwindling as we spoke in depth for another hour. Then crunch time had arrived and it was now the moment to see if he was with me. I put my hand out towards him and asked.

'Are you with me on this Elroy?'

He looked me straight in the eyes and said: 'Do I have a choice Jack?'

What could I say to him? He knew me too well, as I said, he wasn't a fool. I was about to say something when he spoke.

'Will this repay my debt to you Jack?'

'Of course it will and you get a bunce on top as well.'

'Jack, if it wasn't for you, I would not be walking around today. I owe you my life and, no doubt, Rosa feels the same.'

I was now positive he was going to agree and asked: 'Well friend, are you with me on this?'

He paused for a moment, then shook my hand nodding a 'yes' with a loud sigh. I was so bloody relieved when he shook my hand because he was the key to my plan.

'Well done mate, I knew I could rely on you.'

We drank up and left the pub. Outside I told him to stay close to his phone because I would be in touch real soon. Then a funny thing happened as we were going our separate ways. Elroy stopped and turned and called out to me.

'Jack! What would you have done if I had said no?'

I turned slightly as I walked away and replied.

'Nothing mate, because I knew you wouldn't.'

He looked at me shaking his head with a doubtful smile.

'Well Jack, you've known me a long time, so I guess you know me better than I do.'

Of course he knew I was lying; that's why he had asked earlier in the pub 'Do I have a choice?' He knew what would have happened to him if he had said no because he knew the rules only too well.

While driving back, my mind was now going into overdrive. I had a sense of impatience to get this job done and dusted. That was dangerous thinking for me. I had to try and control that type of thought because I couldn't afford to rush things. My thoughts were now on Fred. Would he agree to have Joey whacked or would the slippery bastard have something else up his sleeve which could fuck my plan up? It was always hard to work out what went on in Fred's head. I knew he didn't like being dictated to from my make believe Yardie, but £2 million can sway one's thinking, especially a gangster's. That sort of money could not be lost without causing major ripples in the criminal underworld. Word would have soon got out that our Firm was a soft touch for the taking. The other firms would be soon lurking about like packs of wolves waiting to pounce. That's why Fred was in such a hurry to get things sorted. For him, this wasn't all about the money; it was about respect and he couldn't afford to lose his.

I went to a phone box not far from Fred's house and gave him a ring.

'Hello Fred, can I pop round to have a word?'

His was calm and collected when he answered: 'Have you got something for me then Jack?'

'I have mate, but only if you have something for our friend.'

He was short and to the point: 'Be here at nine in the morning Jack.'

'Nine it is then Fred.'

As I got back into my car, I knew that I wouldn't get much sleep that night because my brain was racing. I had to try and keep the impatient thinking under wraps because I had come too far now to fuck up. When I arrived home I parked the car in the garage and cleared the plastic sheeting from the boot and put my gun away. I was so relieved that I never had to whack Elroy. Apart from the fact that he was a good pal, I was now sick of killing. It was the nonce that had put the icing on the cake for me. Killing someone is one thing, but torturing someone to those lengths is another. The odd bit here and there was acceptable to me if it was to get money or teach someone a lesson, but what I'd done to that maggot was sick. As I entered the kitchen from the side door, Han was at the sink washing-up.

Hannah was really chirpy when she saw me come in.

'Hi Darling, you okay?'

'I'm sweet babe, is Junior in bed?'

She laughed and said: 'Of course he is, look at the time.'

I was miles away and had not noticed the time. It was now ten-thirty and the day had flown by.

'Sorry Han, it's been a bit hectic.'

She stood there drying her hands and was smiling at me with that sweet face of hers. I only had to look at her and I would melt. To me she was the most beautiful woman on the planet. Not only was she the mother of my son, she was also my best mate and lover. I loved her from the bottom of my heart. Her illness had brought us very close together when I really thought I was going to lose her. It was during that time she managed to get under that suit of armour of mine and get to the real Jack and I loved her dearly for that. She had brought something out in me that no one else had ever been able to do, not even my ex-wife. I had never felt real fun and laughter before because my world was always so unreal. It was a world where it was necessary to keep up an impenetrable front of heartlessness. Being seen as happy was considered a weakness by those around me, and believe me when I say those bastards would have honed in on me if they had seen an inkling of happiness.

'Go in the living room darling and I'll make you a cup of tea.'

I was relieved when she said that because she never asked me about my evening. Han was learning pretty fast that I was on a tricky piece of work. I had been acting differently compared to how I worked normally and I knew Han had picked up on it. I knew she hated not being part of what was going on and left in the dark, but I had to keep her and Junior safe. This was where our trust in each other was being tested to the maximum. After all, she was putting all her trust in me. Han had never done anything like that before because she was always an independent person. When we first got together she made it clear to me that she was not a dogsbody like some of the other women that were on the Firm.

We spoke at length about Goa that evening, making plans for our visas and flights. This was where Hannah could come in useful. She could sort all that out and it would give her the feeling that she was doing something. It was arranged that we would get open air tickets which meant we were able to leave at any time. There were the visas to sort out, of course. These could take up to two weeks to get hold of. Also we had to get in touch with some of my friends out there to arrange for our accommodation.

I was right. I never did get a good night's sleep. I ended up tossing and turning until Han told me to fuck off downstairs. I watched the sunrise that morning as I sat at the table in our kitchen. I was mesmerised by it, as it slowly began to rise above the horizon. My thoughts were now more focussed, having used the methods taught to me by the old Guru in India. Having that 'me time' always put my thoughts back in order. I had broken down my whole plan bit by bit, making sure I hadn't forgotten anything, and so far it was going well. Having a daily stock check helped me to put things back into perspective.

I arrived at Fred's house at ten to nine – I was always a good time keeper and hated others who weren't. Fred's wife Cheryl answered the door and invited me in. She was a quiet and reserved sort of person in her mid forties; well dressed and very attractive. She was slightly refined with her accent but never used it to give an opinion. In other words, she was another one who was under Fred's control.

'How's Hannah and little Jack, Jack?'

Hearing her say that always made me smile because it sounded as if it was a stutter or an echo.

'They're sweet Cheryl and doing good.'

'I am so pleased for you both what with Hannah and you having had it so hard recently.'

I liked Cheryl, not because she asked after my family, but because she was the only one out of all the wives and girlfriends of the Firm that stuck by Han and me. When Han and I first got together it caused lots of gossip mongering among the women. They objected to the age difference saying it was immoral and they tried to treat Han as a kid. My Han was having none of it and pulled each one of them up about talking about us. Since then it's been all quiet. Eventually she was reluctantly accepted into the wives and girlfriends club. But the truth was Han didn't want much to do with them anyway.

'Where's Fred Cheryl?'

'He's on the phone in his study Jack. Take a seat in the lounge and I'll fetch you a cup of tea while you are waiting.'

I sat there in this huge room full of neatly arranged antique furniture and oil paintings. The carpet was a cream coloured thick shag pile and you sunk into it as you walked on it. Fred was a collector of anything old and his collection was worth a fortune. Surprisingly, none of it was hooky and had all been bought legit. I could hear Fred shouting down the phone from his study and I thought whoever was on the other end was causing him to lose the plot. Cheryl came back carrying a silver tea tray and sat it down on the table in front of me and started pouring. I asked her: 'Who's Fred bollocking Cheryl? '

'It's Joey, Jack… you will no doubt hear what has happened anyway.'

I was all ears now and wanted to know what the lunatic had been up to.

'What's happened then?'

She was now sitting opposite me and I saw a look of near disgust come over her face as she handed me my tea. I thought, just for a moment, *'Am I making her look like that or what?'* Then she said: 'He's been seeing one of the girls at the massage parlour and Lynne has found out.'

Lynne was married to Joey and was Fred's eldest daughter. She was a spoilt bitch and a daddy's girl through and through. I wanted to hear more of this not just because I hated Joey, but more important, this was all good stuff that could help Fred make his mind up as to whether he was going to agree to whack Joey. I nearly choked on my tea when she blurted that lot out.

'Fuck me Cheryl, is he bloody insane? What did he think he was doing?'

Cheryl sighed as her face took on a more composed aspect.

'I do not know Jack, but Fred is furious.'

'Is that Joey on the phone now then?'

'No Jack, that's Tommy who runs the girls. Fred seems to think that he knew about it and let it happen.'

Acting surprised, I said: 'Surely he can't be blaming Tommy. He must know that he was shit scared of Joey.'

'I know that Jack, but perhaps Tommy should have feared Fred instead?'

She had a point there. Fred would blame Tommy because, in his mind, it was him that *had* to be feared; not Joey. Again it was down to the respect thing and, as I have already mentioned, respect was what it was all about.

Just then Fred came out of his study and stood in the doorway of the lounge dressed only in trousers and vest with his hands firmly placed on his hips, puffing at his fat Cuban cigar. Cheryl quickly got up and left the room via another door leading into the kitchen; probably because Fred was blocking the doorway. She knew well to steer clear of him after he had gone into one. That left just the two of us. I carried on drinking my tea waiting for him to speak. I had learnt from experience never to start a conversation with Fred when he had the hump because he would say that you were telling him what to do or think.

'Come in Jack.' he said as he turned and slowly walked back into his study.

I followed him through his cloud of cigar smoke with my tea in hand and sat at his desk. Fred was seated on the opposite side in his big leather swivel chair.

'Have you heard then?'

'Yes Fred, Cheryl has just put me in the picture.'

Fred looked at me as if I was transparent; he seemed to be looking right through me. He could give a look that was hard to read which gave you the misgiving that he might be able to tell what you were thinking.

'Not good, is it Jack?'

I took a bit of a gamble when I said: 'Well it's not looking too good for Joey, is it Fred?'

Fred just gave me a glare.

'What you got for me then?' he said, changing the subject.

'I've got a shipment of coke coming in worth two million, plus the buyers' dough.'

'Do we know who the buyers are?'

'No Fred, they're a bunch of northern monkeys. Not much to worry about.'

Fred leaned forward in his chair so that his forearms were now resting on the desktop and, with a smirk on his face, he said: 'Not like you to be so cocksure Jack?'

He was right. I had come across too confident with that answer and he picked up on it straight away.

Quickly I replied: 'I had them checked out. They're a little firm from Manchester working the skag around the housing estates.'

Fred looked at me with his smarmy *'You don't know a thing'* expression and then said: 'Well maybe we should branch out into that type of business ourselves. Because it sounds like a nice little earner if they can afford to put up a couple of mill.'

I knew Fred was working me so I had to keep focussed and not make another stupid mistake. Nodding my head in agreement, I replied: 'Maybe we should Fred.'

There was a short silence then Fred said: 'Okay Jack, I've made a decision. We're going to go along with what your Yardie is asking.'

Relieved, I replied: 'Right you are then. I take it that includes Joey in your decision?'

Fred's face changed to a very serious, no nonsense, don't-give-a-fuck frown as he leaned back into his chair clasping his hands.

'Yeah it does Jack and I've decided that Joey has to go.'

That was good news for my plan because it meant Fred had not come up with another one of his own.

'Do you want me to take care of it?'

'Yes and do it very discreetly in your own way okay?'

I had got what I needed, but I had to remember that I was now retired from the Firm which meant I got paid for any work I carried out for them.

'How much is it paying Fred?'

Fred sat and unclasped his hands and formed them into fists. It was hard talking money with Fred because he was a greedy bastard and a shrewd one to boot.

'Hundred grand.'

I was impressed with that figure because I was only expecting about fifty or sixty grand. I pretended to ponder over what was on offer to give him the impression I was rolling it over in my head. But the truth was his offer was more than I expected, especially from Fred. What he didn't know was that I would have done it for fuck all, with or without my plan, because I hated the bastard.

Calmly I replied: 'That's fine Fred, but how much for getting this work organised?'

I pissed him off asking that.

He roared: 'That's all part of your fucking job description Jack! Now, don't take fucking liberties.'

I decided to act like I would normally which meant me not always accepting everything, even with Fred. I spoke with a slightly forthright, raised voice but not high enough to piss him off.

'Fred, we had a deal and that was: I got paid for the hits and anything else I did for the Firm. I'm not on the payroll any longer because I'm now retired from the business, remember?'

Fred took a deep breath then tutted as he got up from the table and walked over to the drinks cabinet.

'What you having Jack?'

'No thanks Fred I've still got a cup of tea.' I said as I raised my cup.

Fred poured himself a large brandy and then returned to his chair.

'Okay Jack, this ain't negotiable. I'll give you another twenty grand on top.'

I sat there and thought about it for a couple of minutes as I would normally do. I didn't take the piss and push for more because I had been extremely lucky up till now.

Fred sat impatiently waiting for my answer.

'Okay, I'm happy with that.'

Of course I was bloody happy! That extra twenty grand would go towards our little nest egg.

'Have you got all the info on this work Jack?'

I looked at Fred and thought for a moment, *'If only you knew that all this was fabricated bullshit'.* Then I answered: 'I'd only been given the basic mate. He wouldn't give it all over until you made up your mind with what you wanted to do with Joey. I'll get back to our friend and give him your verdict and get the rest of it. Then I'll get back to you Fred.'

'Okay, but I want everything: date, times the lot. Do I make myself crystal clear Jack?'

'As clear as daylight Fred, but he's still going to want his money up front.'

Fred got quite shitty with me and remarked: 'I know that Jack. Leave that to me; you just get on with getting the info.'

He was pointing his finger towards the study door for me to leave as I got up to go.

I wasn't happy with his reply. I stopped after a few steps; I could feel Fred's piercing eyes on my back.

Fred asked: 'What is it?'

I turned to face him and answered: 'Well Fred, what do I tell him then?'

'Tell him that I want all his info, and then he can have his money.'

I let out a sham laugh which was meant to give the impression that I didn't approve of the idea. It was then that I started to wonder if Fred did have another plan up his sleeve after all.

Fred just sat there looking at me not saying a word.

I broke the silence and told him.

'I'll be wasting my time if I go back with that answer mate.'

Fred started to get angry with my stubborn attitude and stubbed out his cigar in his brandy. Almost threateningly, he said: 'Listen to me. Considering I've just been stung for two million by his firm, do you really expect me to hand over that dough just on his say-so alone?'

I stood my ground with him and said: 'Yes Fred, I did expect you to do that.'

He just stood there looking at me speechless with his mouth wide open. I was adamant he mustn't get his own way on this because I wanted that money up front and tucked away in my offshore account before the shit hit the fan. I knew he was trying it on with me so I had to play act a role back to him which had me pretending to plead with him.

'Look Fred, I've done my best on this one mate. You can't expect me to go back to him and tell him to simply give over all the info on this work and then we pay him. He won't swallow it mate. He's probably thinking that you won't give him the money because he wants Joey whacked.'

Fred knew only too well that I was right, but he hated losing face. I knew from experience that Fred was a bad loser, especially when doing business. If you were unfortunate enough to be trading or bargaining with him, then he had to be seen to be the better businessman. Most would let him win; not because he was better but because they feared him. Like a spoilt kid, Fred had to be coaxed into parting with his cash. So I had to take my time and make it look like he had made the decision himself without any help from me. What I was doing was very risky because I was blatantly conning him. If he had any inkling that I was bullshitting then I would end up a dead man. My determination to get out of the Firm was so overriding that I knew I had to take risks to achieve it. Dealing with Fred was very dangerous, but my thoughts of Hannah and Junior gave me the confidence to follow it through.

I reminded Fred that he was in the process of getting his two million back and, if that meant putting up two hundred grand, then it would be worth it. Fred was being a self-righteous asshole by giving me a lecture on organised crime and how it worked.

'I know how the game works Fred; I've been involved in it since I was a kid and I've learnt over the years that sometimes it doesn't always go the way we want it to.'

We carried on with what I will call our one-sided debate for another hour letting him think he had won every round. Then it came to crunch time.

'It's your choice Fred, what do you want to do?'

Pointing his nicotine stained forefinger at me he said: 'I'll tell you what we are going to do Jack. Give him half now and the other half on delivery, alright?'

I knew this was the best I was going to get out of him. I told him that I would try to get him to accept the deal.

He was full of himself now and was acting like an arrogant prick, prancing around his office thinking he was businessman of the year. If I'd had a piece on me at that moment, I would've used it to blow his fucking head off.

'You will do better than try Jack. It's your job to make sure he accepts it, understand?'

Manipulating Fred wasn't that hard considering he had a degree in psychology. I knew him well enough to know that he had a big ego problem although he couldn't see it himself. To get Fred to play ball, all I had to do was give his ego a boost. I did that by letting him think he was always right.

'Let's have the cash then Fred.'

'When are you going to meet him?'

'I'll try and sort a meet out for tonight.'

Fred said: 'Okay, but make sure it's out of our manor. I don't want any of our boys seeing you.'

'No worries Fred. I know a good place; nice and safe.'

As Fred left his office to get the cash, he called out to me from the hallway: 'By the way Jack, I want to be there when you have the final meet with the Yardie, okay?'

I couldn't believe my luck when he said that. I had been devising a plan to have him and Joey at the meet and now he was inviting himself along.

A few minutes later Fred returned with a small black leather holdall. As he got within a few feet of me, he threw it at me. Catching it, I said: 'You've told me to deal with Joey my way Fred.'

Fred gave me a suspicious look and answered: 'Yes I did Jack, why are you asking?'

This was to be the tricky bit.

'Well, even though we're giving the Yardie the dough, he's still going to want proof of Joey being whacked.'

Fred gestured for me to sit down again and said: 'Carry on.'

'You've said you want to be there, so why don't we get Joey there as well. Then I can whack the prick in front of our Yardie mate. That way we get what we want and he gets the other half of his dough and sees Joey get whacked. Then we part company happy, except for Joey that is.'

Fred sat very quiet and in deep thought. As I watched him, I was wondering what was going on in that crazy head of his.

The silence was broken when Fred said: 'Where would we meet?'

My heart was racing now because my plan was going so well.

'I know a place out of the way in Surrey Fred.'

Fred pulled himself upright in the chair and leaned on the desk.

'Too far away for me. If it went tits-up, I would need a decent alibi, so it has to be somewhere where I can cover my own ass.'

I said: 'Does that mean you're up for Joey being at the meet then?'

'Might be Jack.'

I said to him: 'What about the north side of the river then?'

Fred stood up and walked across the room, then stopped and turned to me.

'No we'll meet him locally.'

I shook my head in disapproval and said to him: 'You can't be serious Fred, right on the manor?'

Fred smirked.

'Right on the manor Jack. Then that way the rest of the Firm will think it was an outside hit.'

I thought about what he said for a minute and soon realised that his idea was pucker for my plan. It would be looked like a hit from another firm. It was widely known that Joey was none too popular with a lot of our rivals, so the rest of our Firm wouldn't be thinking that one of their own had done the deed.

Then the cunning bastard said: 'We'll have to talk over the contract again Jack.'

I knew the sly bastard would come up with something like this and I knew what was coming. Trying not to let on that I knew what he was up to, I said to him: 'Go over it in what way?'

Fred smiled at me.

'The price Jack, the price.'

I smiled as well and said to him: 'What have you got on your mind then?'

Fred's face changed into a cocky *'I'm fucking smarter than you'* look. 'Fifty grand, is what is on my mind Jack.'

I gasped aloud.

'Fifty grand Fred, you can't be fucking serious. I won't do it for that'

'Look, if I'm there at the scene then I'm as liable as you are to a nicking.'

'I know that Fred but…'

'No buts Jack, fifty it is, right?'

I knew at that moment that things had been going a bit too well. Now this conversation with Fred had cost me dearly and saved Fred a lot. I had planned it for him to be there, but I didn't plan on Fred cutting the contract fee. I had to accept the fifty grand loss to keep focussed on the job in hand. After all, it might seem a lot of money, but it was a small price to pay to get out of the Firm.

Reluctantly I agreed.

'Okay Fred you've got yourself a deal, but for one thing.'

Fred gave me a look that could kill.

'Well spit it out then.'

'I want my money up front, the same as our Yardie mate.'

Fred stared at me with the same hard face and then it cracked into a smile and put his hand out to me.

'No worries Jack, you got yourself a deal.'

Fred had the look of a victor. He had won the day by saving himself fifty grand but unbeknownst to him, he had just set himself up to meet his maker.

Chapter Eight

'Confession'

I arrived home and stashed the money in the garage and then walked through the side door which led into the house. I found Hannah sitting at the kitchen table in silence. I stopped in the doorway and looked in on her; she was facing away with her petite back to me. The room was dead silent, which was most unusual for my Hannah because she always has something on the go, be it the washing machine or the tumble dryer, any room with Hannah in it was never quiet. I stepped into the room expecting her to greet me, but she stayed silent and staring straight ahead of her. Just by looking at her I could tell that she was upset.

'What's up babe?' I asked.

She didn't respond and just sat there not moving a muscle.

I walked around the table so that I was now facing her and leaned on the table.

'Han… Han! Snap out of it! What's wrong sweetheart?'

She looked up at me, her face still giving off that cold glare. I asked her again, this time speaking more softly.

'I won't ask you again… now what's all this about?'

Hannah got up and stepped towards me and shouted:

'Or what Jack? What are you going to do… kill me? After all, that's what you do isn't it? You're not just a villain are you Jack?'

I rushed over and grabbed her by the neck and put my other hand over her mouth. Pushing her up against the wall, I growled in her ear.

'Why don't you speak a little louder and let the whole street think I'm a murderer you fucking idiot.'

Hannah was having none of it and brought her knee up into my bollocks, while simultaneously scratching and punching my face. The shock and pain of that blow loosened my grip on her and put me down on the deck. She then made a grab for our big cast iron stewing pot, probably to smash me over the nut with. I was in agony, cupping my balls with my left hand and as soon as I saw what she was after, I made a grab for her ankle. I pulled her leg as hard as I could and she lost her balance, falling backwards onto the floor next to me. I pulled on her leg and dragged her right up close to me and threw myself on top of her. I'm a heavy set geezer and my frame has held down the best of the tough guys out there on the street. However, Hannah was a different breed and fought like a maniac. She wriggled and squirmed trying to free herself from my grasp. It took all my strength just to hold her until she calmed down enough for me to get my breath back and for the pain in my balls to recede.

'Stop it Hannah, I don't want to have to hurt you.'

She made one more attempt to free herself but I was too strong for her. Finally, she gave up the struggle, relaxed her body and turned her face towards mine and said deliberately: 'It's true isn't it Jack?'

I could smell and feel her breath, we were that close.

'Is what true Han?'

'Cut the crap Jack, I know when you're lying.'

I gathered she must have heard something about me and the contract killings. Whatever it was, it must have been good enough to convince her that I was a killer. I had never seen her like this before, so I knew it was serious. I asked her to calm down so that we could talk in a civilised manner at the table.

'Okay Jack, but you must promise to tell me the truth.'

I looked at her with my face now covered in blood and replied: 'Okay babe, I promise.'

As we got to our feet, both of us were breathing heavily. I felt like I had just had a fight with Mike Tyson. Who would have believed that Hannah had just kicked the shit out of me?

'Sit down and I'll fix your face.'

I knelt down and picked up my gold bridge and placed it on the table. Han turned from the sink and looked at it and then at me.

'I'm so sorry Jack; I didn't mean to break your teeth.'

I just stared up at her, not saying a word, as she came over to me with a bowl of hot water.

Hannah had never seen me really angry before. But here, she had tested my patience to the extreme and I had to be careful that I didn't lose control and retaliate.

Han was now gently bathing my face; the water in the bowl had turned red from my blood. There was absolute silence apart from the sound of dripping water as she rung a handkerchief out over the bowl. Anybody seeing this situation wouldn't have believed that she had been responsible for what had occurred only a few moments before.

'Where's Junior?'

'At my mum's. I didn't want him here while all this was going on.'

I asked her again: 'Are you going to tell me what all this is about?'

Hannah stopped wiping my face and took a step back.

'Do you kill people Jack?'

I tried to get more information out of her because she had me put on the spot.

'Who's put that idea into your head Han?'

'You do, don't you Jack? Otherwise you would have said no.'

I picked up a towel and started to dry my face. Han was just standing there waiting for an answer. I could have tried denying it but she would never have attacked me if she thought her information wasn't sound. We had made a pact when we first moved in with each other that we would always be honest with each other. I put the towel down and told Han to sit down. I had decided to tell her the truth and my only hope she would understand my reasons for doing it.

'Yes babe, I kill people.'

Han slowly sat down opposite me; her face looked shocked.

'I never had a choice Han. It was either that or a bullet in my skull.'

Han was sitting there open-mouthed staring at me, not saying a word. I leaned over and took her hand. She looked down at our hands clasped, then looked straight at me. I gave her a gentle squeeze and tried to remain as calm and measured as possible.

'It's really true then; you do kill people. Haven't you got a conscience Jack?'

I needed her to understand that I was not as cold-blooded and callous as she was thinking.

'Of course I do and it's having one that has got me putting this plan together. It was never just about me retiring babe because I can't; they won't let me. I had to compromise and ended up agreeing to whack a few people per year. That was Fred's idea of a pension plan for me.'

Hannah squeezed my hand and said: 'Why didn't you tell me about this Jack?'

I laughed painfully and answered: 'Because sweetheart, your life would have been at risk. Maybe Jack Junior's too.'

She let go of my hand and sat upright in the chair.

'Why would my life be at risk Jack? It's not me going round killing people'

'Look at it this way babe, if you divorced me or you shacked up with another geezer, do you think you could just walk away having all that info on Fred and me?'

'What do you mean? Are you telling me that you would kill me?'

'No, I couldn't kill you babe, that's why I kept it quiet. But that wouldn't stop Fred or Joey. Anyway, who told you?'

'Maggie.'

I was confused now and said: 'Maggie? Who the fuck is Maggie?'

She answered: 'Maggie, who works at the parlour Jack. You know the one: mid twenties and very pretty with the long blond hair.'

Angry at what she had told me, I raised my voice: 'How the fuck would Maggie know that I've been nipping out every now and then whacking people, I've not told a fucking soul!'

Han apologised for not telling me sooner and then said: 'She has been having an affair with Joey and I suppose he has been telling her all the Firm's business.'

I looked at Hannah in disbelief and asked her if she knew if Maggie had told anyone else.

Han said: 'I don't think so Jack.'

'If she has, then she has probably signed her own death warrant.'

'What do you mean? Is someone going to kill Maggie? She can't help what Joey says to her.'

'It's not Maggie I'm worried about… it's you I'm concerned for.'

'Me? What do mean? I haven't done anything apart from listen to her.'

I explained to her in more detail that Fred would be none too pleased if he got wind of Maggie's big gob. Knowing Fred as I do, he would probably have her and anyone else she has told whacked.

'This is like a bad dream, what am I going to do?'

'You're going to do fuck all Hannah because pretty soon we'll be out of the manor and long gone.'

'I know how it works Jack. They will kill my family if they can't get me. You know I'm right Jack.'

'Listen to me babe; I ain't got time for this right now because my fucking mouth is killing me so I'm going to the dentist. I'll speak to you when I get back. In the meantime, contact Maggie and get her ass round here and put her wise. Keep her here till I come back okay?'

I left Hannah in the kitchen and made my way to the dentist. My thoughts were now on Maggie; I wondered what she actually knew. But my priority was to shut the silly bitch up and try and save her life. Fred had already got the hump with her for shagging Joey and he wouldn't think twice about having her whacked. To him, she was just a slag with a big mouth and in Fred's world those types of people were scum and he would have no qualms about having them removed permanently. This situation wasn't looking good because it could cause problems, not only for my family, but also for my plan.

After the dentist I belled Hannah.
'Hello babe, did you get hold of Maggie?'
Han sounded really excitable.
'Yes Jack and she's really frightened.'
'Well, keep her sweet until I get there.'
Hannah spoke with concern in her voice.
'She is going to be alright Jack?'
I answered her honestly.
'I hope so sweetheart, I'll do my best for her.'
'What are you going to do for her?'
'I'll talk with you when I get back babe, just keep her sweet okay?'
'Okay, don't be long darling.'

I needed to know who else Maggie had talked to about me. She was known as a chatterbox, like some of the women connected with the Firm. What I didn't need was this getting back to Fred, I needed to whack the bastard first.

Arriving home, I went in through the kitchen and noticed my blood on the floor and the kitchen was still in a mess from our fight. My mouth was still numb from the jab I had at the dentist and I had been dribbling a little. I made my way through into the lounge to where Hannah and Maggie were. On entering the room Maggie stood up dressed in a short mini skirt and a revealing top and walked quickly up to me and nervously said: 'I am so sorry Jack for talking about you; I swear I have only told Hannah and no one else.'

I asked her: 'When did you get told that I kill people Maggie?'

Her eyes appeared like saucers and she stepped backwards.

'Don't be scared Maggie. I'm not here to hurt you sweetheart okay? Just tell me when?'

She looked around at Han, who was standing by the fireplace, for assurance. Reassuringly, Hannah said: 'Maggie, just answer the question for him honey.'

Maggie turned to face me and said: 'It was about a week ago Jack.'

I asked her how and by whom.

She explained that Joey had come back to their love nest really angry, saying something about a meeting going wrong and him getting all the blame for it. She went on to say that he was slagging me off big time, saying that I was Fred's ass licker, along with the story of me being the Firm's hit man.

Hannah went over to Maggie and made a joke about me being a hit man. Her idea was to make Maggie believe that it was all bollocks because Joey had been pissed off with me. Maggie went on to say that he used to tell her loads of stuff, but she thought a lot of it was made up because she found it too hard to believe.

I gathered from what she was saying about Joey getting the hump at a meeting that it must have been when we were at the Firm's office. Fred had bellowed him out and made a mug out of him. He must have been desperate to talk with someone when that happened, but who could he go to? There was no one, not even his wife, because she was Fred's daughter and everyone else had something to do with the Firm. Choosing Maggie as an earpiece was stupid – if Fred had found out, he would have had him whacked for sure. So, poor old Joey was doomed from the start. Whatever way things went he was to end up dead either way.

I focussed back on Maggie.

'Sit down Maggie and listen to what I am about to say to you.'

She was shaking as if she had a chill. I gestured at Han to sit down next to her, just to make her feel less scared.

'Listen Maggie, you have to be really honest with your answers, I don't want any bullshit okay?'

There were only a few questions I needed to ask her. I crouched down in front of her and said: 'Apart from Hannah, who else have you told about me?'

She had already said she hadn't told anyone else, but there was always a chance she might have fibbed. She hesitated with her answer and that meant she was lying. Han picked up on it and put her arm around her shoulder and said: 'Maggie, if you have told someone else, then tell Jack; he isn't going to get angry with you for not telling him earlier.'

Maggie was looking scared and started to cry. I took her hand and gently stroked it and reassured her that everything would be okay. She looked at Han then me and went back and forth looking at each of us several times. Then finally, she blurted out: 'Tommy!' I told Tommy!'

I caught eye contact with Hannah and the look she gave me was one of fear. I was in a spot now because Tommy was already in the limelight with Fred over his alleged knowledge of Joey's affair.

I focussed back on Maggie.

'Okay sweetheart, well done for being honest with me.'

She was wiping her tears away and said in a near on naughty schoolgirl voice: 'Am I in trouble Jack?'

I let out a soft sigh.

'No Maggie, no one is going to hurt you.'

Getting back to business, I asked her: 'Listen Maggie, have you got family or friends you could go and stay with while I sort all this out?'

Maggie eagerly replied: 'I could go and stay with my sister who lives in Dover.'

I inquired: 'Does Joey know where she lives?'

'No Jack, we've never discussed my family.'

'Right, this is what I want you to do Maggie. Go home, pack a bag and get a taxi to the railway station. Give Hannah a ring when you're on the train, okay?'

Hannah came up to me whilst Maggie was on the phone to her sister and asked me what I was going to do next. I told her I'd have to think this through and while I did that, I wanted her to make sure that Maggie got underway sharpish. Hannah decided to take Maggie back to her flat to help her pack and put her in the cab. The two of them went, leaving me to my thoughts. I had to go over my options and not let anything be left to chance. This plan of mine was going to be life-changing, as well as life-threatening. My thoughts were on weighing up the pros and cons and coming up with the best solution.

The facts were that Maggie had opened her big mouth to Tommy. So, should I take a chance that he hadn't let it out of the bag to someone within Fred's earshot. I also had to consider carefully what Fred might do if he did get a whisper of this gossip from the criminal grapevine. As I said before, Fred was no mug and would never take any unnecessary chances, especially if it meant his liberty could be at stake. It could be possible that he would put Joey's contract on hold and postpone the meet with our phantom Yardie. He could get the idea that his name might get a mention if the Old Bill happened to get involved in the allegations about me. If that became the case, then he definitely wouldn't want to get himself connected to Joey's hit. If that happened, then my strategy would've been fucked and Han and I would be back to square one.

It took a couple of hours for me to come up with what I was going to do. My thinking was now ruthless, which meant I wasn't prepared to take any chances that could fuck my future plans up. I had made a decision to pay Tommy a visit to find out from him if he had opened his mouth to anyone else. I would be hoping he hadn't because it would make my job easier.

Hannah came hurriedly through the door kicking her shoes off as she scurried along the hallway leading into the lounge.

Breathing heavily she said: 'I done it Jack ... she's now on her way to the railway station… she will be on the *Three Ten* and will ring you when it leaves… How's your mouth darling?'

I felt my pride kick in and gave Han a scowl and ignored the question.

I asked: 'Did she want to go Han?'

Han had picked up on my mouth and sussed I was pissed off, so she left it and replied: 'Of course Jack, she's pretty scared, especially when she realised that Fred could be after her.'

'That's good because that's how we want her to be: nice and scared; her fear means she'll lay low.'

Hannah warned her not to phone anyone until this blew over.

I liked that in Hannah; she was always on the ball and would think things through. That was her streetwise experience coming into play.

I now had to get to Tommy before Fred had a word with him about him knowing about Joey's fling with Maggie. Tommy lived only a few miles away; living on his own since his missus died a few years back. I had to get to Tommy pretty quickly to sort him out. Then there would be less chance of him gossiping about me being a killer and reducing the chance of the Old Bill getting wind of it. In this business, info like that was like gold dust if it fell into the right hands. If a desperate criminal was in a spot of bother with 'the filth', and things weren't going too well for him, he could use that information as a bargaining chip for a reduced charge or even being allowed to walk. The Old Bill would have thought that they had a mega result and most definitely have done business with him. They would have loved to get their smarmy hands on the likes of Fred, Joey and me.

Hannah came and sat with me and leaned over and gently kissed me on my cheek to avoid my split lip. She gave me a hug and stayed like that for a few moments not saying a word.

I broke the silence and said: 'Do you believe me when I said that I never had a choice but to accept Fred's pension plan?'

She loosened her gentle grip on me and sat upright holding my hand. Looking at me she said: 'Yes Jack I do. At first when I heard it from Maggie, I presumed that you had been doing it all the time you've been at the Firm. But now you've explained, I realise you done it for Junior and me to be able to give us a better life. I do think though, that Fred thinks he is some sort of God, especially the way he controls people's lives.'

I listened intently to what she had said and decided to let her in on the whole plan, including my plans for Tommy. She knew things were getting tricky because of the Maggie incident and it wouldn't take her long to realise that I was holding back on her. That would've pissed her off big time and, to be honest, she was shrewd and clever and could probably give me a bit of advice. My thinking was not foolproof and I had made mistakes in the past that had cost me dearly. As the saying goes, two heads are better than one.

'Han I'm going to tell you something now but I'm not going to have a lot of time to explain. Time is not on our side and I have to act fast.'

Han asked me to briefly explain.

'I'm going to whack Tommy.'

'Wow! Just like that? You mean right now?'

'Right now Han; that's why I can't explain at the moment, but when I get back, I promise I'll come clean and tell you all about my plan, okay?'

'Sure Jack, but do you really have to kill Tommy. He's such a nice bloke.'

I got a bit short with Hannah and barked: 'That's what I have been trying to explain to you! I ain't got time for this right now, but all will be revealed when I get back. Trust me Han, okay?'

With a sad look on her face, she nodded compliance.

I made my way to my stash place, where my guns were kept and grabbed a snub nose .38 special for the job. Han had followed me out and asked me: 'Who's driving for you Jack?'

I was undressing to put my work clothes on.

'Only me babe, don't need anyone else knowing my intentions.'

'Well, seeing that I know, why don't I drive for you?'

I gasped aloud.

'I can't let you do that sweetheart. You're the mother of my kid; what would happen to Junior if it went wrong and Old Bill got involved? You could be nicked as well.'

'Look Jack, we are not going to get caught and if it did go wrong, at least you have a better chance of getting away by having me as your driver.'

I knew there and then that there was no point in arguing with her and apart from that, I didn't have the time. So, I reluctantly agreed.

'Okay sweetheart, but you're only the driver, you don't move from the car for any reason okay?'

Han's sad attitude quickly changed and she was now full of beans and agreed wholeheartedly. I would wonder about her sometimes because she could be cold and ruthless as any man; then she could be the nicest person you'd ever want to meet.

'Remember Han, I'm the boss and you will do everything I tell you to do, okay? There's not to be any rows whatsoever.'

I could tell Han really wanted to get involved. Perhaps that tom-boy trait she had in her was surfacing because she wasn't acting very ladylike.

'Change into an old tracksuit and tear out the labels and wear a cap. We ain't got time to nick a motor, so we'll have to use ours. So, to be safe, I want you to park up a few streets away, do you understand?

Almost like an obedient soldier, she replied: 'Understood Jack.' and shot off upstairs to sort her clothes out.

I had never worked like this before. I knew having Hannah on board would worry me, but it would also ensure I would be extra vigilant.

I was dressed and ready to go, my gun was stashed in its holster and I had stashed a stiletto knife in my pocket. Hannah came running down the stairs just like a school kid in a hurry. That's when I could see her age in her. She often did things that teenagers would do and it would embarrass me sometimes, especially when we were out together in older company. However, she did do her best to act like someone older than her years and she could pass it off really well when she wanted to.

'I'm ready Jack.'

'Good girl, now go and get the Jag out of the garage babe and bring it around to the front. Don't forget to put a pair of those surgical gloves on.' I said, pointing to a box of them on the table.

As we drove to Tommy's place Hannah never said a word. She was doing a good job; acting professional. As we got within a few streets of Tommy's place, I told Han to park up in a slightly obscured part of the street we were in. Once we stopped, I double-checked I had everything and turned to look at Hannah. This girl had always told me that she loved me but I wasn't so sure, probably due to the age difference between us. So I partly held back on showing my true affections towards her. But under that suit of armour of mine was a geezer who loved her dearly and desperately wanted to tell her – every minute. But my pride had a big part to play in it. She was steadily chipping away at it by being so loyal, understanding and loving. I was beginning to soften up and accept that she was genuinely in love with *me* and not what I represented. A lot of the women I've known would love to snap up a gangster, no matter if he had a face like a donkey's ass. It's the bad boy image they represent that turns them on. I needed to know Han wanted me for me and not my status.

As I opened the door to get out of the car, I said to Han:

'I'll be as quick as I can sweetheart, try not to attract any attention to yourself and don't throw your fag butts out of the window either, okay?'

Han gave me an inquisitive look, so I quickly explained: 'If found sweetheart, they give perfect forensic evidence.'

Chapter Nine

'Strictly Business'

I made my way through the few streets which lead to Tommy's house, wearing a hat and keeping my head down. Once I was at his place, I looked around the surrounding area to see if there was anyone lingering about. I had to be cautious like that because anyone lurking about could be a potential eyewitness if things went wrong. I went around to the rear of Tommy's place and made my way through the back garden leading up to his kitchen. I looked through the window but saw no movement inside. I moved towards the kitchen door and tried the door lever; surprisingly I found it to be open. I entered nice and quiet and crept into the passageway, keeping my ears tuned in for any noises. It was then I heard someone cough; it came from the living room which was the next door along. Tommy's place wasn't a palace; a burglar wouldn't get a day's money out of robbing the gaff. You see, Tommy was a gambler and a bad one at that. So as you can imagine his house was quite sparse.

I was at the foot of the door and gripped the handle gently with one hand and pulled my pistol out with the other. I slowly opened the door and was confronted with the back of Tommy's head sitting in his armchair with a pair of old style headphones on watching the horse racing on the TV I thought for a moment should I whack him now, but I wouldn't know if he had talked to someone else. I put the gun away and took my gloves off then walked up to him to give him a nudge.

'Aaaaaahh!' was his first reaction. Then he turned around, pulling his earphones off at the same time, and yelled: 'Fucking hell Jack, do you not use the bell?'

I put a false smile on and answered in a friendly voice: 'I've been ringing that bell of yours for the last 5 minutes Tommy and now I'm seeing you with those Biggles earphones on, it's no fucking wonder you never heard it.'

'What do you want Jack?' he said as he got up from the chair.

'I need a word with you Tommy, that's all.'

Tommy gave me a worried look and said: 'If it's about Joey and Lynn, I can only tell you what I told Fred on the phone. I knew fuck all about their affair'

Tommy was a quiet type of bloke. He was in his late fifties, balding and fat. He had worked in organised crime for most of his life; mainly in prostitution. He wasn't a villain like the rest of us; he was more of a trusted employee.

'Sit down Tommy.'

As he was slowly lowering himself back into his chair, he looked apprehensive and asked: 'Is this where I get a good kicking then Jack?'

I gave him a surprised look and replied: 'Only if you get the next few questions wrong mate.'

'Honest Jack, I didn't know Maggie had been shagging Joey.'

'Look Tommy, I'm not here for that bollocks; it's something else I want from you.'

'What's that then?'

'Did Maggie tell you anything about me?'

Tommy's face changed into a very worried look.

'We both did, especially when Hannah was ill, but that's it Jack. I never spoke out of turn or bad-mouthed you. I have the greatest respect for you. Has someone been telling you different?'

I was surprised with Tommy because he wasn't mentioning what Maggie had said to him about the hit man rumour. I thought he must know that was important, so why wasn't he mentioning it?

'Okay Tommy let's try another one. Did Maggie tell you something about me that she had heard from Joey?'

Tommy went as red as a beetroot and started to swallow hard. These were good indications that he was lying and knew what I was on about.

'Listen Jack, Maggie was pissed and rambled on about some nonsense about you being a hit man.'

'And what do you think about that Tommy?'

Shrugging his shoulders he said: 'It's none of my business Jack'

I asked him: 'Has Fred seen you yet?

'Do you mean for the affair business?'

'Yes mate.'

'Only on the phone.'

'I'm over there tonight Jack, and I'm praying he will accept that I knew fuck all about it.'

'Tommy one more question; have you told a living person that I am a hit man?'

'No Jack, I have not told a soul.'

I just carried on looking at him not saying a word. He started to get really agitated and blurted out: 'Honest Jack, not a soul.'

I had already made up my mind what I was going to do with Tommy. I had never seen him under pressure before, and if what I had just witnessed was anything to go by, then he would have had me shitting a brick if someone like Fred or the Old Bill got hold of him. The Old Bill would've got the lot out of him, maybe all of it, in less than five minutes. Fred would've whacked him as soon as he showed signs of sweating because he could smell fear and if you were fearful in Fred's eyes, then you were as good as buried. He had become a living liability to me and he could bring all my hard work and planning down around my ankles. Then I'd be fucked.

'Calm down Tommy I believe you mate. Go and get yourself a towel because you look like a wet sponge mate.'

'I'm not sweating because of being nervous; it is because I'm ill Jack.'

As he left the room, I pulled my gun out of its holster and put it in my pocket for easy access.

Tommy had come back wearing another shirt and had put some aftershave on to cover the stench of his body odour.

'That feels better, now I've had a cool wash. I think I've come down with a virus.'

'Yeah you already said mate. You want to get yourself down to the quacks first thing; to get yourself sorted.'

I was trying to pacify him and give the impression that all was sweet and after a bit more crap chat between us, I made my excuses to use the toilet. I had decided that this was where it was to happen. I left him in the living room while I went upstairs. In the toilet I put my gloves on and glanced at myself in the mirror. There was determination written all over my face. The sight of my reflection even made me wary – my eyes especially: they looked frightening, almost evil. Lots of people I had known over the years have said my look was very scary, especially if they were on the receiving end of it.

I fucked around with the flush handle on the toilet system to create some noise; enough so that Tommy would hear. After a few minutes of making a racket, I heard Tommy shout up from the living room.

'Are you having problems with that handle on the cistern Jack? Hang on mate. I'll come up and sort it out for you. I heard him to climb the stairs and he even started to whistle as he neared the door. He tapped on the door and said: 'I'm coming in Jack?'

I opened the door and he stepped back to let me out, muttering something about the cistern under his breath. I watched him as he had his back to me and knelt down to get better access to the now broken lever. I pulled the gun out of my pocket and pointed it at the back of his head. Tommy was oblivious to what was happening behind his back and carried on effing and blinding as he attempted to fix the toilet. I was completely focussed on the job in hand at that moment. I looked down at Tommy and thought: *'this isn't personal mate, it's strictly business.'* I took one step forward and. at the same instant, grabbed hold of his hair tightly, and forcefully smashed his head down hard on to the top of the cistern, splattering his face. The force from me jammed his head against the wall and I held it in position. I then rammed the barrel of my gun right into the back of his neck and fired. Bang! Blood shot out from the front of his throat and splattered on to the tiles in front of him. He fell more downwards then forwards probably because he was shot through the neck. A shot in that area does not create much tissue resistance when the bullet enters. If it had been in the chest, the bullet would have acted more like a sledgehammer blow probably knocking him back because of the amount of bone and muscle.

Tommy ended up kneeling with his head in the toilet basin. He was in his death throes and making gurgling sounds. Parts of his body were going into spasm, twitching and jolting like he was having shock treatment. There was a huge amount of blood pouring from his throat. I knew from experience he was still alive, but unconscious. I looked at the blood splattered wall and noticed a hole. The bullet had gone right through Tommie's neck and exited out through his throat and embedded itself in the wall.

Finally, there was one last sharp movement from Tommy and I countered it by pushing my knee even harder into his back to keep him over the toilet basin and to stop him from falling to the floor. I wanted him to bleed to death rather than putting another shell into him. The noise of the first shot had made a racket and I didn't want to make more unnecessary din. There was one last deathly gasp from Tommy and experience told me he was now dead. I took my knee away from his back and he slumped to the floor facing up at me, eyes wide open. The damage the bullet had done on exiting his throat was devastating, there was a hole the size of a fifty pence coin where his Adam's apple used to be. Bits of veins and shreds of pink flesh were hanging out of the wound.

I got my knife out and dug the spent bullet out of the wall so I was not leaving evidence about. I moved out of the bathroom and went downstairs just to make sure that I hadn't dropped anything and to cover my tracks before leaving. I stashed my gun and checked in the mirror to make sure there were no blood splatters on me and, when I was satisfied, I left the house via the same route I had arrived and made my way back to Han.

'Wasn't he in Jack?' Hannah said once I got in the car.

'Just drive the motor and head to a car wash.'

Hannah said no more and drove the two miles to the car wash in silence. Once we were on the conveyor and the car was being swamped with soapsuds, Han ask me again: 'Was he out Jack? And what are we doing in here? Shouldn't we be trying to find him?'

I looked around at Hannah and said: 'It's done Han, now get me home so I can burn these clothes.'

Hannah was really surprised with that answer and said: 'Done Jack? That was bloody quick, what happened?'

I gave her a look that I reserved for thick people and replied: 'I fucking shot him Han, what did you think I done?'

She cautiously carried on inquiring.

'I never heard nothing, no shot or loud bang.'

Speaking patiently I said to her: 'Hannah sweetheart, you're not meant to hear fuck all.'

Hannah could be quite naïve sometimes; she had no idea on how a hit was performed.

She was now buzzing and kept asking me questions about the hit on Tommy and the others I had done in the past. She even seemed to be getting turned on with the thought of having a partner who was a killer. I could never work that one out because, a little while ago, she was so anti-hitman that she tried to crack my skull open with a cast iron cooking pot. But now she was practically having an orgasm when I spoke about it.

I changed the subject and got back to my plan.

'I want you to drive back home via the river sweetheart.'

Hannah turned and gave me a funny stare. I knew she was dying to know why we were taking the detour, but she didn't ask; probably to give me the impression that she knew what it was all about. The fact was she was doing everything how it should be done. If I had been using a driver on a piece of work then his job was driving and nothing more. No questions, no fuck all; the driver just did as he was told.

We were now driving along the embankment parallel with the River Thames. Hannah asked me where I wanted to go. I told her to head for Chelsea to where the houseboats were moored. The traffic was beginning to build up and I wanted out from this side of the river before the rush hour kicked in. I never did like being in this manor on this side of the water, nor did I like the breed of villain that the area produced. They were mainly foreign or yuppie con men who weren't my cup of tea.

'This will do sweetheart, just pull up over here.'

When she had parked up close to the houseboats, I told her to stay with the car as I wouldn't be long. I got out and walked along the edge of the river and stepped up onto a wooden pontoon which was out of sight of the road and the other houseboats. I pulled the gun out of my pocket and threw it a good thirty feet into the Thames. I had been at this location many times over the years dumping all sorts in the river. I would often wonder what would happen if they drained it. Just imagine; they would find everything from a morgue full of corpses to an arsenal of weapons.

Chapter Ten

'Keeping up a front'

As we made our way back home, my thoughts were now on Fred. He would be expecting me to turn up tonight with the moody info from our phantom Yardie. I told Hannah all about Elroy and the plot to kill the pair of them. She was one hundred percent behind me and even tried to justify my reasons for doing it. I had to laugh at her because I would have bet a million pounds that she wouldn't have wanted to get involved and help me out, especially with a couple of hits. Here I was, telling her everything; something I had never done before because I never trusted anyone. All the work I was given by the Firm was generally carried out by me alone because it was safer for me that way. Now it seemed I had taken on a partner and so far, she was doing okay.

Once we parked in the garage I stripped everything off and told Hannah to do the same. As we stood there completely naked I could see Hannah's eyes transfixed on my cock. She smiled and walked towards me and I knew what was coming. I could see Hans's nipples were fully erect and knew she was turned on. She knelt down in front of me and took my now throbbing cock in her mouth and began to suck and lick very gently, at the same time, cupping my balls with her left hand. I knew I would come really quickly if she carried on doing that, so I lifted her up and held her at waist height where I entered her while she clamped her legs around my waist. I moved her up against the wall where I could push my throbbing tool into her harder and, picking up speed, we got into an ecstatic rhythm. Han was crying out with pleasure as I pumped away into her shaven haven. She let a loud scream out as she reached orgasm, the feeling of her cum running down my shaft made me so excited, that I exploded into her already soaking-wet pussy. As I let her down onto the floor, she straightened her legs and a sticky line of my cum dripped out of her in one long strand nearly touching the floor before breaking off. Making love to Hannah was amazing because she could turn every switch on in me. Sex with her was fantastic; I'd never met anyone that could satisfy me like she could. To me, she was my own sex goddess. We both looked at each other and said at the same time *'I needed that'*. We even managed to get a laugh out of it while it lasted.

Now though, it was time to get back down to business and get the next stage of my plan underway. It was then that the phone rang and Han took it. She whispered to me that it was Maggie and she listened for a moment before passing it over to me. I said: 'You're late sweetheart.'

She told me that she couldn't get a signal but was now at her sister's. I told her not to contact anyone except Han and me and only if it was an emergency. She asked about Joey and Fred but I told her to think about herself and just lay low until we contacted her. She thanked me and told me how grateful she was. I passed her on to Hannah who said her goodbyes and ended the call.

Hannah said: 'She seems okay now that she is out of the way.'

I said: 'As long as she doesn't contact anyone or come back to the manor, she'll be fine.'

I asked Han about the visas for India. She told me that it was all sorted and they would be with us within a few days. I told her to start transferring money from our stash into our offshore account, just leaving us a few grand as pocket money. She said that she would sort it all and then asked me about Tommy.

'What is going to happen when Tommy gets found?'

'Well let's put it this way sweetheart. The Firm will put it down to Fred – for Tommy not letting on about the affair. Fred will think it's Joey for the opposite reason, that Tommy had been shooting his mouth off. And the Old Bill will put it down to a gangland hit.'

She said: 'That's cool. That means we are in the clear then? No one can point the finger at us can they darling?'

'No sweetheart, they can't and don't forget we had to whack Tommy to protect our plan and our future. He wasn't our enemy and never forget that Hannah. The only reason why Tommy was taken out was because he became a liability. Think of it as business and not personal, okay?'

Hannah nodded a *yeah,* then got inquisitive once again, asking: 'Is that what you had to do with the others that you killed Jack?'

'Of course I did, otherwise I wouldn't have a conscience. A pretty limited one I'll admit. But better than none at all.'

That evening I had got myself mentally prepared for my meeting with Fred. Arriving at his house, he greeted me at the door and told me to wait in the lounge and help myself to a drink. I could hear Sammy's voice coming from the study, but couldn't hear clearly enough what was being said. As I sat there with my brandy, the door of Fred's study opened and Sammy appeared.

‘How’s it going then Jack?’

‘Not bad Sammy, how about you?’

‘I’m on a mission mate. Tommy has gone missing.’

‘What do you think’s happened then Sam done a runner?’

‘He would be fucking silly if he has Jack. You know what the outcome would be if that was the case.’

I said to Sammy: ‘I’m sure he’ll turn up sooner than later because he ain’t the type to have it on his toes. I reckon he’s gone to ground because he’s shitting himself about Fred, that’s all.’

It was obvious to me that Tommy was still where I left him and I knew it would only be a matter of hours before they would go and kick in door and find him. All I had to do was act like nothing had happened because, in theory, it was none of my business.

Sammy told me that he had the boys out searching for him and was sure it wouldn’t take long before they collared him.

Fred came in to the lounge and said: ‘Has he told you about Tommy?’

‘Yeah Fred, but as I said to Sammy, he’ll turn up.’

‘Thing is Jack, that slapper Maggie has done a bunk as well.’

I laughed and said in mock surprise: ‘You’re not saying those two have done a bunk together Fred?’

‘Well it’s beginning to look that way.’

I was getting impatient now and wanted to get Fred on his own away from Sammy and get on with the next stage of my plan.

‘Look Fred, with respect, I ain’t that interested in Tommy or Maggie. I need to have a private word with you.’

I knew that would piss Fred off talking the way I did, but I needed to bring a sense of urgency to the situation to give the impression to Fred that I was on the hurry-up.

Stony-faced, he looked right at me and ordered: ‘Okay Jack, you mind your manners and apologise to Sammy.’

I thought *‘you cheeky bastard’*. He’s getting me to eat humble pie just for asking for a private word with the flash cunt. He got pleasure from embarrassing and belittling people; he thought it gave him a God-like image because we all did as he asked.

Humbly, I faced Sammy and said what Fred wanted to hear.

‘Sorry Sammy, didn’t mean any disrespect mate; I just have some important business to sort out with Fred privately, that’s all.’

Sammy smiled. He knew the score on how Fred worked. He could see I was complying under duress. He didn’t want an apology from me and knew it was only Fred getting his own entertainment at my expense.

‘No problem Jack, I was just on my way anyhow so no disrespect taken’

Fred butted in: ‘Just remember your place Jack. Do you understand where that is?’

‘Yes I do Fred; loud and clear.’ I said under pitted breath.

Fred walked Sammy to the door giving him instructions on how to find Tommy. He walked back into the lounge and sat opposite me and said: ‘What was all that about Jack?’

I knew he was referring to what I said: ‘Sorry Fred, it just came out the wrong way mate, no disrespect intended.’

He looked me up and down which made me feel like a mug and I could sense my blood boiling because this prick was now beginning to get to me. I could’ve taken Fred apart with my bare hands; he wasn’t a fighter because he didn’t have to be. He was a clever bloke with plenty of clout who had other people do his dirty work for him; that’s why he was the boss. Reluctantly, I would just have to swallow my pride and be tolerant of the fucker.

‘That’s okay Jack, just don’t let it happen again. Now I hope you got some good news for me.’

‘I have Fred; I’ve been to see him and got near on everything for the Charlie deal. It’s a straight swap, cash for coke at a warehouse over in Leytonstone.’

I got Fred’s attention now.

‘When is it to be Jack?’

‘In a week.’

Fred smiled like a spoilt kid and asked: ‘How many of them will be at the meet?’

‘Four, they kept it to a minimum Fred, which is pucker for us.’

‘Will both Firms be tooled up?’

‘It’s a dot on the card that they will be. Probably only be small arms. They won’t want to bring attention to themselves carrying anything bigger.’

‘What’s your thoughts on it Jack?’

‘Well Fred if it was my work, I’d have four on the job all with AK’47’s and piss this bit of work. In and out in five minutes.’

Fred started pacing the room back and forth with his right hand cupping his chin. This was a habitual mannerism when he was thinking.

Then he said: ‘It makes sense having a bit of artillery there. Ensures we bag the goods.’

‘Did you get the times sorted?’

‘Yes mate, I’ve got the lot except the exact address of the warehouse where the deal is going down.'

'What's he doing? Hanging on to that until we sort Joey out?'

'Yeah, he'll give that over when we meet to give him the rest of his dough along with Joey.'

'Are you completely satisfied with this whole set up Jack? You're not getting any of those gut feelings of yours, are you?'

'I'm sweet with it all Fred, no gut feelings.'

'Good, I'll sort the men out for the work. How about you, do you fancy some of this Jack?'

'Let's not go over that again Fred because you know where I stand on that, but I wouldn't mind having my money.'

Fred let out a laugh and said: 'Don't trust anyone, do you Jack?'

I looked back at him, smiled, then replied: 'Of course I do – when I get paid Fred.'

He laughed at my dry wit and promised to sort the money out in time for the meet, then asked: 'Any more thoughts on how you're going to sort Joey out?'

'Yes Fred I have and I'll do it when we meet the Yardie. What have you told Joey about what's going down?'

Fred's face coloured as he barked: 'I was trying to put the idiot in the picture when all this shit about him having an affair came out. But leave him to me and I'll sort him out.'

I then mentioned the obvious.

'What are you going to do with Tommy when you find him? You do realise we can't afford any bother while we've got this going down.'

Fred came over to me and stood that close to me I could smell his breath as he said: 'Don't you worry about Tommy, Jack. I just want to teach him a lesson in respect, that's all.'

'Okay Fred, you're the boss.'

'I know that, but he seems to have forgotten don't you think?'

Changing the subject I said: 'Right then Fred, I'm going to sort out the meeting place and I'll keep it close to the manor – you okay with that?'

'Well done Jack, but keep it nice and close; I don't want to be out of my patch if this goes tits up.'

'Alright mate I'll be touch in a few days.'

I got into my car and made my way home, thinking over the day's events. I decided it was time to get in touch with Elroy to clue him up on what was happening and stopped at a phone box.

'Hello mate, Santa wants a word with you.'

Elroy let out a laugh and joked: 'I'm fucking too tall and the wrong colour to be an elf Jack, how are you mate?'

'Good mate, good… listen, we need another meet. You free tomorrow?'

'Yes Jack, but you'll have to come over this side of the river because I got a lot on.'

'Okay Elroy I'll be at your office at seven.'

'Is everything still sweet then Jack?'

'Sweet as a nut mucker; see you tomorrow.'

Going over to Elroy's office at seven would mean that the pub wouldn't be that busy. I hated crowded places and always felt uncomfortable with the noise that comes with it. Perhaps it was a form of being insecure because I felt I had less control of the situation when out of my comfort zone.

As I came through the door, Hannah greeted me with Jack Junior in her arms. I hadn't seen much of him over the last few days and it felt good to be with him with my favourite lady – and now my new partner in crime. Han was good like that. She would always make sure that I had lots of contact with Junior, even if it was only for a few minutes. She would say it was important to keep us all close. She put Junior down for the night while I ate my dinner downstairs with some light classical music playing in the background. The music helped me to relax and slow my thinking down. Hannah appeared at the doorway and asked me how things went with Fred. I explained that Tommy had still not been found and that Fred had the troops out looking for him.

'By the sounds of it Jack, it won't be that long before they find him.'

I looked up at Han and said: 'Fred would go berserk if that were to happen. Knowing Fred as I do, he would definitely blame Joey and would probably shoot the fucker on the spot.'

Han replied: 'We don't want that to happen, do we? We need him at the meet with Elroy?'

The truth was we really couldn't afford for that to happen because if he whacked Joey, then our meet would be fucked up and our plan would be out of the window. I now had to give this some serious thought.

'No we don't babe, let's hope Joey stays at home with Lynne.'

Han made a good point when she mentioned that. She went on to say:

'You'll have to stay close to the Firm now. Until Tommy is found Jack, just in case Fred goes around to Lynne's and starts on him.'

Of course she was right but what she didn't take into account was that Fred was unpredictable and impulsive. It was bad enough that Joey had caused Fred to lose face by shitting on his daughter. Fuck knows what he would do if he thought Joey had whacked Tommy. If it was the case that he thought Joey was part of Tommy's death, I had to hope he would wait till I whacked him, according to our plan. So, I decided to take Han's advice and hang about with the lads till Tommy was found, and hopefully be there to sort Fred out so he didn't fuck up our strategy.

After dinner Han and I went and sat in the lounge. We spoke of our future plans together and what we would do once we got to India. She spoke of opening up a restaurant and fresh juice bar. I joked and said that I could nip up to Rajasthan to sell weapons to the rebels. She actually believed me and I had to promise her that it was only meant as a joke. It did make me laugh that I could wind her up so easily. She would say that I had a hard face to read which meant that she couldn't tell if I was being serious or joking.

I had my sights on buying some land to build a holiday complex with a huge pool, shops and amusements, both for the foreigners and Indians alike. It would generate enough money and, compared to the UK, it would represent a small fortune. In the past I had lived out there like a king on two hundred pound per week because everything was so cheap. Every fucker is on the take out there and if I had any problems, there would always be someone willing to sort it out for you for a small donation. That's why I loved the place; it was like home from home. I slept well that night having made my plans for the following day to spend time with the boys and meet Elroy.

Chapter Eleven

'Joey's Work'

The next morning I made my way over to the snooker hall. This was where the lads would meet to start their day. This snooker hall business was one of the Firm's smaller enterprises and it became not much more than a meeting place for the Firm.

As I climbed the steps I could see Benny was talking to Mike at the other end of the dimly lit room. They were in deep conversation, so I let them be and went to the bar, ordered a cup of tea and waited. After ten minutes the pair of them shook hands and turned to see me up at the bar. Benny shouted from the other end of the room: 'Hello Jack how are you mate?'

I said loudly back: 'I'm okay mate and how about you?'

'Sorted Jack, now that Mike has done the business for me.'

I jokily said: 'Well seeing you've had a result, you can get the breakfast in.'

Mike followed us through to the cafe area where we all sat and started talking about what had recently been happening with the Firm. I needed to know from these guys, rather than Fred, what was really going on.

Mike started talking about Joey.

'He's fucked himself big time now by shagging that old tart Maggie.'

I was all ears listening to this when Sammy mentioned that Fred was sending the boys in to Tommy's place that morning.

I added a bit of dry wit to the conversation.

'Why? What do you think he's doing? Hiding under the kitchen sink?'

Sammy laughed and said: 'Knowing that cunt, he's probably hanging from the rafters.'

We sat there and debated about what we thought had happened to Tommy. I dropped an intentional bombshell when I mentioned that perhaps Joey had topped him because he probably knew a bit too much about his antics.

'Fuck me Jack, you're probably right about that.' said Sammy

Mike added: 'Yeah and I heard a while back that Joey has had a few old tarts from that parlour going in and out of that flat he was using.'

This little chat we were having was paying off for me. Already I had put the seed in their heads that Joey could be responsible for Tommy's disappearance. I was also taking the dairy off me when his body was finally found. It would be important for me when the *'Who dunnit?'* hit the streets. I had never had a public beef with Joey. Even though I hated the prick, I had kept my feelings about him quiet, whereas the others on the Firm would often slate the fucker while his back was turned. So I was sure I wouldn't come under suspicion when it all came on top.

As we were eating breakfast, one of the girls from the kitchen came over to Sammy and whispered in his ear.

'Won't be a moment boys, got a phone call.'

He got up and made his way to the back of the kitchen, after which Mike said to me: 'Sounds like something's up Jack.'

I carried on eating and just murmured: 'Could be mate.'

Sammy came back from behind the kitchen counter and made his way back to our table. Without saying a word, he started to put his coat on. Mike was looking at him as if he was waiting to be told something, but Sammy was silent and in deep thought. Finally, Mike blurted out in frustration: 'For fucks sake Sam, what's going down?'

Sammy looked at the pair of us and suggested we take this outside and made his way to the exit. We quickly followed and once we were outside in the car park, Sammy turned to Mike and me and said: 'We've found Tommy.'

Mike said sarcastically: 'Where has the dodgy fucker been tucked up, then Sammy?'

'He's been blown away Mike; looks like he's been there for a few days.'

Mike remarked on our earlier conversation: 'That's Fucking Joey's work, the mad bastard!'

I spoke up and said to the pair of them: 'Careful boys, don't start Chinese whispers about Joey because you could come unstuck.'

I pulled Sammy to one side and asked Mike to stay back while I had a private word with him.

'What are you going to do Sam?'

'Don't know yet Jack, I've got to think this one through. Have you got any ideas then?'

'As it happens mate I have, but get shot of Mike first so we can take a drive and try getting this sorted. Instruct your boys to keep staunch and, whatever happens, don't say fuck all to Fred or anyone else ...well not just yet anyway, okay?'

Sammy gave Mike his car keys and told him to go home and wait for a call from him and, above all, say fuck all to anyone. Mike didn't even question his given orders and just nodded, got into the car and drove off.

I commented to Sam that Mike took that well.

'He knows this is serious Jack, especially now he thinks Joey could be involved.'

That made sense to me because most of the Firm were fearful of Joey.

Sammy and I drove off away from the manor and I knew what I had to do with him. That was to try and delay Fred getting wind of Tommy's death. As I've already said, Fred was an unpredictable bastard and could blow the whole plan. No amount of money would stop Fred from kicking off if he thought someone was taking the piss. He would without doubt believe that Joey would have been responsible for Tommy's death, and that paranoid, twisted brain of his would tell him that Joey had something to hide. Joey wasn't exactly flavour of the month in Fred's eyes and it was my job now to get this work with whacking the pair of them done as soon as possible.

Sammy said: 'What you got on your mind then Jack?'

I inquired: 'Who found Tommy?'

Sam said: 'Mike's boy. He's sound as a pound Jack and is still at Tom's place waiting on us to let him know what to do next.'

'Bell him and tell him to lock up and go back to his Dad's place and wait'

Sammy was insistent: 'What's all this about Jack. Why can't I just tell Fred?'

I had to think fast here because he just asked the million dollar question.

'You know that Fred has been working us to get his £2 million back?'

'Fucking right I do Jack. He's been like a man possessed since he got turned over.'

I began working Sam with my patter.

'Fred and Joey have come up with a plan to get it back. I don't know the full details, but what I do know is, if Fred thinks Joey is responsible for Tommy's death, then there's a good chance he will lose the plot and fuck Joey over there and then; without any warning. If that's the case, it will mess the plan up and the onus is going to full back on us to come up with something to get his precious dough back.'

'When is this bit of work meant to happen then?'

'Pretty soon mate, maybe a couple of days.'

Sammy's reaction was kind of comical when he said: 'Poor old Tommy, he's going to be fucking honking by then.'

I got a bit short with him and abruptly said: 'Well, roll the cunt up in a carpet and spray it with *shake and vac* or something. Just use your loaf. This deal has to go down before Fred is put in the know about Tommy.'

'Okay Jack, keep your hair on. I'll keep this under wraps for as long as it takes and I'll tell Fred I am still looking for him. Just let me know as soon as this deal has gone down. Come to think of it, why don't any of us know about this deal?'

I pointed out that he and a few of the others had been working with Joey when he got turned over.

Sammy wasn't amused with what I had just said.

'Are you saying he doesn't trust us?'

'I'm not saying a word Sam but you ain't got to be Einstein to work it out mate. I think he wants to keep this as low a profile as possible, lessening the chance of something happening.'

'He is a slippery cunt is our Fred.'

I replied: 'That's why he's the boss mate.'

Sammy asked me if I thought it was Joey who killed Tommy. I took my eyes off the road and looked at him, then said: 'If you want my honest opinion Sam, then I'd say yeah, he had the motive. If Fred had got hold of Tom before Joey then who knows what Tommy might have told Fred?' Joey was playing with fire when he fucked about with those girls at the parlour. He became the victim of the 'power of the pussy.'

Sammy said: 'Makes sense mate because Tommy had no enemies, he was just a 'Yes man'; not like us.'

'We'll find out soon enough after Fred gets his money back, but if he finds out that Tommy is dead before that happens, then this Firm will explode. So it's important to keep schtum.'

I dropped Sammy off at Mike's place telling him that I'd be in touch as soon as I knew what was happening. I then drove to a car park I knew in North Dulwhich. I had been considering this place for the hit and wanted to look at the place in daylight to weigh it up a bit more. It was not far from Fred's home and had a wooded area at the edge which blocked the view from the main road. I knew this location would keep Fred sweet. I had decided to use an Uzi machine gun on these two with the intention of unloading the whole magazine into them; that being one hundred 9mm shells in a matter of seconds. I had designed their execution to have all the hallmarks of a Yardie hit because the Uzi was their weapon of choice. Basically, they were useless shots, but give them one of these weapons and they couldn't miss their target blindfolded. The gun had no accuracy from distance, but at close quarters it would spray bullets across a wide spectrum, hitting anything and everything within twenty metres. These weapons were regularly used in the States for drive-by shootings, but the only problem was, they not only got their target but any unlucky civilians that happened to be in the vicinity.

I drove into the park which was empty apart from the odd jogger and a few dog walkers. I looked for a good place from where to carry out the hits. There were two parking lots that had about fifty car bay spaces right opposite each other with a thirty metre space running between them, a bit like a no-man's-land. I pictured Fred, Joey and me on one side of the parking lot and our phantom Yardie, Elroy on the other side. I sussed out quickly how this bit of work should go down and came away satisfied with the knowledge that I had found the perfect spot for Fred and Joey's demise.

I arrived home just as Hannah was opening up our mail and I could see she had an envelope from the Indian embassy.

'Is that our visa's babe?'

'Yeah, but they're only for six months, we'll need longer than that.'

I explained to her how the Indian visa system works which took away her confusion. I said to her. 'Well that's all our travel documents sorted.'

I asked Han if she sorted out the accommodation. She told me my mate Raj had sorted out a villa in a place called Calangute in Northern Goa. I knew the area well and thought it would be a good place to re-start our lives. This was a massive step for both of us and, to be honest, I was so used to plans going wrong or changing, that I thought the same might happen with this one. Everything had gone so well up till now that I kept thinking to myself that someone or something might throw a spanner in the works. It was as if I was expecting something to go wrong. Han spoke and brought me back down to reality. She was talking about our furniture and everything else in the house.

'What are we going to do with all our stuff Jack? Come to think of it, what are we going to do about the house?'

I like to think of myself as a clever geezer, but like I said earlier, having two heads is better than one. I had totally forgotten about the obvious things, like the house and furniture. I had not made any preparation at all. That was probably due to the fact that I thought something would go wrong with all the planning and living this double life.

I owned up to forgetting everything about the house and then she suggested to me that she should do more to help. I agreed with her and told her more about what had gone down.

'Bloody hell Jack you are a genius and a madman, especially fronting Fred like you have because that takes guts on its own.'

I told her that I couldn't afford to make any mistakes because a lot of thought had been put into this and, if that qualifies me to be a genius, then great. But she was right; I had to be a madman to carry it out. I also told her that this was our last chance to be free and happy.

Han laughed and said: 'Don't get all sentimental on me Jack. Let's get back to the here and now. So, what are we going to do?'

'Maybe we can rent or sell the house.'

'That sounds good. Perhaps we can rent it through one of those agencies who take care of everything.'

I nodded and agreed.

'You leave all that to me and I'll sort it out, okay?'

I left her in the kitchen and took a shower while Han made some grub for me. My thoughts were now strictly focussed on the set-up in the car park. This bit of work had to go down as quick as possible before our Fred found out about Tommy.

As I sat and ate, Hannah came up behind me and gave me a cuddle and told me that she loved me. She was always affectionate and showed her love for me often. I had, at the beginning of our relationship, been very conscious of the difference in age between us, but she put me at ease when she said that she preferred older men because they were more reliable and affectionate. Even her family, except for her Mother, were okay about our relationship. I found out quickly Hannah had been out with some right scumbags who had beaten and verbally abused her. She had to learn quickly that she would have to stop this happening, so she learnt to fight back. She had never been shown affection before by any of her previous lovers, but with me it was different. I would tell her daily that I loved her and I always told her that she was beautiful. Unbeknownst to me, Hannah had a bit of a reputation as an easy lay when I met her, but that was because of the age gap and scene. We hung out in different circles and places, so I wouldn't have known anything about her. I only found out about her past after I'd fallen in love with her, but to be honest, it was too late by then; she had me hooked. When I fell for her, I managed to get myself to believe that I didn't care about her history because that was in the past, and what we had was a new beginning for both of us. I knew she loved me and was being honest when she told me. I was streetwise for fucks sake and knew what we had was very special. People were not too inclined to tell me that my bird had been about a bit because they knew they would've ended up on a mortuary slab. As far as I was concerned, she was as good as a virgin and I treated her with respect; not like the mugs she had been with before.

I left for my meet with Elroy at his office. Once there, I entered the bar area and found it to have less than a dozen punters which suited me fine. I went straight into his office without knocking and found Elroy sitting in his chair with a bird crouched between his bare legs giving him a blow job. She pulled away and looked up at me with shock written all over her face. Elroy however, wasn't that amused and asked me to give him ten minutes, and then pushed the girl's head back down on his throbbing black cock.

I smiled but never said a word and shut the door. I went up to the bar and ordered a brandy. After twenty minutes the office door opened and the girl came out as if she was late for a plane. She kept her head down and made for the exit. I could tell that she was embarrassed. Elroy came to the door entrance just dressed in jeans and sweatshirt. He beckoned me to come into his office and I got up off my stool at the bar, bringing my brandy with me. As I got close to him, he told me to go in and give him five minutes to take a piss.

The room smelt of body odour and cannabis and, on the side of his desk, was a used condom. I looked around the room and went over to the window to open it up to let some fresh air in. Just then, Elroy's huge frame came through the door, cutting the light out from the bar area. 'Sorry about that Jack, I was just giving the bird an interview.'

I had to laugh but felt sad for her as well because the girl was a good-looker and could have been model material or at least something better than a prostitute. Like so many from the wrong side of the tracks, she was to become a fucking brass, letting all sorts of scum fuck her for fifty quid a throw. Elroy puts his hand out to me to shake hands. I looked at his hand, then turned my head to look at the condom on the desk, and then focussed on him.

'I'm not shaking that hand mate, so you can put it away.'

He laughed at me and went and sat in his chair, pulled a big spliff from the drawer of his desk and lit it, exhaling a huge cloud of smoke.

'Okay, what's happening Jack?'

'It's all sorted mate, and will be happening in the next few days. I've got the pair of them at the meet and it's in the car park I mentioned.'

Elroy took another long drag on his spliff, coughed and then said: 'Where am I situated then?'

'Exactly where I said, mate. You'll be about fifty metres away from them and, apart from one street lamp, you'll mainly be in the shadows and not that noticeable.'

'I take it I get paid when the job's done Jack.'

'As soon as I carry out the hits and we're safe, okay?'

'That sounds good enough for me Jack, but what happens if something goes wrong mate, and you have to have it on your toes. I'm out of pocket aren't I?'

I had been thinking about a Plan B, if things went pear-shaped. I had to think of Hannah and Junior before myself. What would make me feel better was, if I could get Han and Junior out of the way as soon as the hit went down. If it went wrong, then she could get herself to India and I could join her at a later date. If it went right, I would want her here at home to act normal when the questions were being asked because it wouldn't just be the Firm; it would be the Old Bill as well. Our plan was for Han, the boy and me to walk off into the sunset without being sussed.

I thought of something that would work both for Elroy and for Han and me as well, so I decided to run it by him.

'I've got an idea mate; I'll give Hannah the money and she will pay you when you see me whack the pair of them. However, if it goes tits up, then you've got to get my Han and Junior to the airport. You'll get your dough when she has checked in. That okay with you Elroy?'

Elroy got up, shut the window and turned to me and said: 'You must trust her lots man, because you realise she'll be a witness to two murders. What will she be like in a few years' time mate if you two fall out with each other? She could use it against you Jack.'

I didn't want to explain to him that Hannah was now my partner and couldn't use anything against me, if it ever came to that. So I just said: 'Leave that to me to worry about Elroy.'

I asked him if he could get a motor for the work and if he could, had he got his Rastafarian outfit?

'Yeah man, got the outfit, but what sort of motor… a sporty one with plenty of poke?'

I dismissed his idea.

'No mate, forget about the sports cars. Just get me a family-sized estate car or people carrier 'cause Han will have Junior and our bags with her. If it went pear-shaped, she would need to get away a bit sharpish. If that happens, we need to make sure that her, Jack Junior and all their stuff can be transported to safety.'

Elroy smiled and said to me: 'You are a clever man Jack and, if you were a businessman, then you would be chairman of ICI by now.'

I had to laugh at him, but I *was* here for business. We thoroughly went over what had to be done for the night in question. I didn't want to leave until I was 100% sure that he knew what he had to do.

'For fuck's sake Jack, I know what I have to do. Stop treating me like a muppet mate!'

For a moment I forgot all about the plan and the reasons why I was there with Elroy. I didn't like his last remark because it pissed me off being spoken to like that.

I looked over at Elroy and said to him with that no-nonsense look of mine.

'I'm going to give you some sound advice Elroy.'

Elroy sat there looking at me; I could tell he knew he was out of line for his last comment and quietly said:

'What's that Jack?'

'You want to watch it with that shit you're smoking my friend, because it makes you sound as if you're a boss talking down to his foot soldier. With an attitude like that you could find yourself in serious trouble. Do we understand each other Elroy?'

Elroy's face had changed from the cocky know-it-all look to a passive near on grey colour, once I had finished giving him my words of wisdom.

'Sorry Jack, I didn't mean to disrespect you man. I do realise that you just wanted to get things done right. You're probably right; I smoke far too much of this shit.'

I leaned over and spoke within two inches of his right ear.

'Well don't let me find out that you've been smoking that shit on the night, especially with my Han and Junior in your motor. You understand what I'm saying Elroy? You protect them with your life if things go wrong; you understand?'

'I won't Jack; I'll be on the ball. I give you my word on that, okay? Anyway, you should know that I would protect your family.'

I changed my facial features to a friendlier one and patted him on the shoulder and said to him: 'That's good enough for me mate. Now go and sort a car out and make sure it's a newish one. I don't want one that's going to break down.'

Eagerly, Elroy started kissing ass and said: 'I'm on it tonight Jack and I'll have it rung by the morning.'

What Elroy meant about having the motor 'rung' was the car had to be stolen then changed a little; like putting on another tax disc and a set of number plates that were registered to an identical car, same make and model and same colour and year. So if the car got stopped by the Old Bill, then it would check out on their computers as not stolen. I wanted one more thing from Elroy and that was the Uzi, which I knew he could lay his hands on through his own Yardie contacts.

'I can get it for you Jack, but it's going to cost.'

'How much are we talking here mate?'

Elroy started rubbing his unshaven chin and said: 'To you Jack, three grand.'

I let out a laugh and told him to pull the other one. I repeated the question again.

'Okay Jack, two grand and that's as low as I can go.'

I agreed and explained that I wanted the large magazine containing one hundred rounds.

I told Elroy to contact me the next day to confirm he had the gun and motor. I left him there and made my way to the car. I sat inside and turned on some Mozart. It helped me focus on my thinking and slow it down. I had been multi-tasking which can be mentally exhausting, so I had learnt to take that 'me time.' I went over everything that had happened so far and it was going so well, I almost believed my own bullshit. This was a very dangerous bit of work I was participating in. It wasn't like putting a shooter to someone's head or breaking someone's fingers for not paying on time.

This work was about conning one of South London's most feared crime bosses and, in the process, killing his psycho sidekick. Then, adding insult to injury, stealing a fortune off him; all without getting caught. The downside to it all would be if I fucked up. Then I'd be tortured and whacked. Hannah would be raped and killed and Junior would end up being put into a bin liner alive and thrown into the canal. So why was I taking all these risks and putting my Han and my kid in danger? It was because we wanted a life where we could be free from the clutches of the likes of Fred and Co. They never gave a flying fuck about me over the years. I'd committed almost every known criminal act for them. All for what? A thousand pounds a week and free meals in the restaurants we were extorting.

We had people saying hello and kowtowing to us, even though they fucking hated us all because of fear. There was certainly no genuine admiration or respect. I had been in this game a long time and seen and done some terrible things, but as I got older, my thinking began to change and that meant doing something about it. Clarity was not just a word for me anymore. Neither were the coincidences that kept happening. The clarity comes when I started to get a conscience. And then the coincidences came to remind of the clarity. It was then that my conscience started revealing more of itself and that's when I decided that I wanted out of this game. I'd met the girl of my dreams and had a beautiful kid. I had been loyal to the Firm, never took a penny I hadn't earned and played the game straight. But as soon as I asked for something for myself, they disrespected me by turning me into a part-time hit man. Did these cunts think I was joking when I asked to retire? Did they think I was like one of their other ass kissers?

I was as clever as the best of them in the world of crime and I could beat them at anything they were up to. A lot of the income Fred had coming in was down to me and I just let him think he was clever. His fucking ego was now going to cost him his life. So that's why I was doing this: to be free with my Han and Junior, to do what we wanted, and go where no one knew us or pissed in our soup.

Chapter Twelve

'Loyalties'

The next morning I felt weird and, for some reason, I decided to go and see Father Malone. I waited for him after he had finished celebrating mass. He was surprised to see me and greeted me warmly as he walked up to his gravel drive leading to his vestry.

'Well, well the saints behold, is this a miracle I am witnessing?' he jokingly said.

'No Father, it's not a miracle. I just thought I'd pop in and see you about Junior's christening.'

I had decided on the spur of the moment, without talking it over with Han, that I wanted Father Malone to baptise him before I sorted Fred and Joey out.

'Come in Jack and tell me how you want to go about it.'

As I entered his study, I could smell the odour of stale tobacco and whiskey.

'Please Jack, sit down and take the weight off your feet.'

Before I could start to talk with him, he asked: 'And how are the lads Jack, staying out of mischief?'

I smiled back at him and said: 'Of course they are Father, don't they always?'

He smiled at me and asked me if I wanted a dram of whiskey.

'As it happens Father, I will.'

He gave me a solemn look and said: How about Jack, has he been behaving himself?'

I paused for a moment and could hear his clock tick in the silence. He got up and went over to his cupboard to get his bottle and poured two glasses. As he handed me my drink, he asked me if I'd had any more thoughts about getting out of the Firm. When he pried with those types of questions, you could almost feel as if he knew the truth of what I was up to; I was sure he had that ability. I found it hard to lie to him and went round the houses without giving too much away.

'That's why I'm here Father.'

He looked surprised and asked me if I had quit.

'No, not yet Father, but I'm about to over the next few days. That's why

I want Junior baptised. I want a completely fresh start for all of us.'

'And have you been behaving yourself Jack?'

I laughed and replied: 'You're worse than my mother used to be.'

But he was persistent and asked me again.

'Look Father, I will be ready for another confession pretty soon okay?'

He gave me one of his knowing looks and said: 'Well my son I have the time right now, shall we start?'

'No Father, don't push me on this one, okay?'

He took another sip from his glass and said to me: 'I understand Jack. So, it won't be long before all is revealed then?'

I smiled and said: 'That's right Father all will be revealed soon enough'

'I know when to keep my nose out of it Jack and from the look of you, this is not the right time is it?'

'You got it in one Father; I have a lot on. Now I want you to sort Junior out and I don't want a soul to know.'

He poured himself another whiskey, but I declined his offer of another shot.

'Surely you are not ashamed of anyone knowing of his Catholic faith are you Jack?'

'No Father, I just want it informal with only Hannah and me being there. Can you get me a couple of Godparents from the congregation?'

'I won't ask any more questions Jack because it's obvious that you have your reasons.'

'When can you do it for us Father?'

'Well my son, I can do it tomorrow for you if you are happy with that.'

I said: 'That's great Father, what time?'

'After nine o'clock mass dear boy.'

I then said to him: 'What time will that be then Father?'

He shook his head in mild disappointment.

'That answer Jack, tells me all I need to know about how long you have stayed away from the Church.'

'I'm sorry Father, but I'm doing my best here.'

'I know you are my son. Be here at ten thirty. Does Hannah know of your intentions?'

'Well Father, she will when I get back home.'

I finished my drink and got up to leave, when Father Malone took my arm and stared at me earnestly.

'I have a feeling Jack that I will not be seeing a lot of you in the near or even distant future. Am I right?'

I was amazed at this old priest because he was more of a clairvoyant than a man of the cloth. I just smiled and reminded him of our last conversation regarding me getting away from the Firm.

'God bless you Jack and I will see you in the morning. Give my love to Hannah.'

As I left the vestry and got into my car, I knew that I would be back to him with another confession, only this time I would be justifying it as the right thing to do. I had to doubt that would cut much ice, even in Father Malone's eyes. Well, redemption would be something I would have the rest of my life to ponder.

I arrived home to find Hannah packing boxes of our belongings. I asked her what she was doing.

'What does it look like I am doing?'

'Look sweetheart, if everything goes to plan, we can't be sitting here with all our belongings packed up giving the impression we are about to leave. It will bring suspicion right down on us.'

'Well, what am I meant to do with our stuff then?'

'Leave it; just pack a couple of suitcases in case it all goes wrong and bring them along with Junior on the night.'

'Jack, I'm so scared of being there babe. You know ... when you do your business on Fred and Joey.'

I came over to her and gave her a big cuddle and whispered in her ear.

'Han darling you won't see a thing, I promise you that. The only reason why you're there is if it goes wrong, then you and Junior will be able to get out of the country quickly, before the Firm start trying to track me down.'

She looked up at me and smiled and said: 'I love you so much Jack, you are the only bloke I have met that has been good to me and I don't want to lose you.'

I gave her an extra hug and replied with greater conviction than I actually felt: 'Hannah darling you're never going to lose me. I have put too much effort and hard planning into this and I know it will work out for the both of us. We *will* live that life that we always dreamed of.'

Han then changed the subject.

'Jack, where have you been so early? You were gone when I woke up.'

'I went to see Father Malone Han. Junior is being christened tomorrow.'

Hannah looked at me startled and then she began to get angry and said: 'Tomorrow Jack, how the hell do you expect me to get things organised by then?'

Speaking quietly I replied: 'Han, you don't have to, because it's going to be a quiet affair, okay? No one there except us, not even your mother and

I don't want an argument about it, okay?'

'But why? Why can't we have a proper christening?'

'We can at a later date, but not tomorrow.'

With tears now rolling down her cheeks she kept on at me.

'But, why can't we Jack? Please tell me why.'

'If I tell you babe, you might get upset'

'Tell me Jack.'

'Okay Han I will, but don't you say a word, right?'

She nodded her head in agreement.

'When this bit of work goes down, there could be repercussions if it went wrong. What I mean by that is that you, Junior and I could all end up dead. I don't what my son meeting his maker without being christened; it's a sin. That's why Hannah, it's just a precaution, that's all babe.'

She stayed silent as promised. I could only worry that she might throw a tantrum because I could see she was really angry with what I had done. I changed the subject and asked her if she has sorted all the money out and moved it over to our offshore account.

Standing with her hands on her hips she said sarcastically: 'I have done it all Jack. Paid in that money that was in the bag and left us five grand just in case of an emergency. Just as you wanted.'

'On the night Han there's going to be another wad of cash meant for the Yardie along with my whack for topping Joey. I want you to pay Elroy out of that and the rest we will stash here so we have an emergency fund.'

She came over to me and put her arms around me and snuggled her sweet face into my chest and asked me if I was scared. I pulled her gently back away from me and looked into her beautiful brown eyes and said: 'Hannah if I said no, then I would be lying. Of course I'm scared. Only a psychopath wouldn't be, and you may think I am one sometimes, but the truth is, I'm not babe. I just want out of this game and to live normally with the two most important people in my life. If it means doing all this to achieve it, then I'm prepared to do it. It's their fucking mistake for not taking me seriously enough when I asked to retire, and it's fucking obvious they think I'm just like the rest of their 'Yes men.'

Hannah said: 'Well they've got that wrong haven't they Jack?'

I looked at her and said: 'They sure have sweetheart.'

Hannah went off to sort out clothes for Junior's christening and I left the house to use the phone to speak to Fred.

'It's about time Jack where the fuck have you been?'

I had to bite my lip and count to ten because he was talking to me like a piece of shit again. I near on bellowed down the phone by saying: 'I've been working Fred. Remember I said I would be in touch with you in a couple of days? Well, I'm now getting in touch with you as promised, so what's the problem?'

Fred was giving it his arrogant attitude and said: 'Don't get smart with me Jack because it don't suit you. Now, are you coming to see me or what?'

'I'm on my way and will be with you in an hour. Is that okay with you mate?'

'Don't be late.' Then he put the phone down on me.

I felt real hatred for this prick now and I was looking forward to pumping fifty fucking holes in his big head. So-called *infamous crime boss*; I've fucking shit them!

Right then I felt a need to be with normal people. I went for a pint in my local and mingled with the lads. It was nice to have a conversation with people who weren't connected to Fred or organised crime. In a way, it brought me back down to earth and reminded me of where I came from. I only had the one pint with the lads and then made my way over to Fred's house. I was feeling less stressed after being with the boys. When I pulled into Fred's driveway I couldn't help but smile when my gaze fell on his Roller. It was still sitting there with the side smashed in and my thoughts at that moment were '*serves you right you flash bastard'*. I got out of the car and saw Fred. He was standing by the door waiting for me.

As I climbed the steps to his doorway, he said: 'Hello Jack, everything okay?'

'Everything's fine Fred, how about you?'

He totally ignored my response.

'Have you seen Tommy on your travels Jack?'

'No I've not seen Tommy for a while now.'

Fred just stayed silent.

I carried on: 'I reckon he's gone to ground. As I said before, he's shit scared of what's going to happen to him from you.'

Slamming the door behind us he blurted out: 'He fucking wants to be scared when I get my hands on him.'

'Look Fred, call the hounds off, give him a few days and I bet you a pound to a penny he will surface. Tommy's not a threat to anyone; he's just scared that's all. I bet my last pound that it's Joey that's put the fear of God into him.'

Fred took me into his study, poured me a brandy and said: 'You think Joey has had something to do with his disappearance?'

'Look Fred, you've got the hump with Tommy for not informing you that Joey was shagging Maggie. Your pride is hurt because Lynne's your little girl. You know Joey is a fucking psycho and you know that Tommy is probably too shit scared of saying anything to you. He's always been loyal to you Fred and never fucked up before. Have you spoken to Joey about it at all?'

Fred picked his drink up and swallowed it in one gulp. He then slammed the empty glass on the table and angrily said: 'The only time I want to see that bag of shit is when you whack him Jack.'

I went on and told Fred that the Yardies' info was pucker and that I had everything worked out for this coming Friday. I had led Fred to believe that there was a pit filled with lime waiting for Joey. Then, changing the subject, I started to talk business with him regarding my money and the Yardies.

'You'll have it on the night Jack, but if the work goes wrong you're accountable for it all. Do I make myself clear?'

I said: 'Yes you do Fred, as clear as daylight, but with respect, I need the dough before the night.'

Fred took a deep breath and rolled his eyes and said:

'Are you sure the take on this work is going to cover my losses?'

I assured him: 'Fred, not only will you have your money back from the Charlie, you'll also have the buyers' dough as well. So either way, you come out a winner. Also, there's a bonus as well: getting rid of that idiot Joey. After all, he's the one that has caused you all this trouble. You'll feel much better after the weekend mate; once you get your crew on it to sort the Yardie work out.'

Fred's face changed into a smarmy miser's grin; I could almost smell the greed in him. He was never happy with enough, he always wanted more and didn't give a fuck what he had to do to get it. He was like a junkie wanting his gear. Fred would go into withdrawal if the Firm wasn't getting enough money from arm-breaking and extortion. He was one avaricious bastard; always had been. This was a strictly business chat and, as far as I was concerned, and I had my own plans regarding when I got paid. An important part of my plan was to have my dough up front and not after the work was completed, for obvious reasons.

Fred puzzled me by completely changing the subject and said: 'You know Jack I want to let you in on something that I have never told a soul before.'

Surprised I said: 'What's that then Fred?'

'I always thought you and my Lynne would have hitched up after your divorce from Mandy.'

I thought to myself *'he's lost the plot'* because his daughter Lynne might be a looker, but she was also a female version of Fred. I smiled and said:

'Thanks Fred, but the truth is I found it hard to get involved with someone else after splitting with Mandy. When I did finally get over the divorce, your Lynne was already shacked up with Joey.

Fred said: 'What the fuck she sees in that prick I don't know because he's been shagging anything that moves.'

I said to him:

'I couldn't do that to my Han Fred because I love her too much. I'm a one woman man.'

'Yeah, I believe you are Jack. You're not like the others. If that lot can shit on their wives then they could shit on me.'

I gave Fred a concerned look and said: 'You okay Fred?'

Surprisingly he said: ''Course I am Jack; I'm just letting you know where loyalties should be.'

I smiled at him then said: 'So Fred, can you sort my money out?'

'I tell you what Jack, you can have it now.'

I smiled and jokily said: 'You sure you're alright?'

Fred poured some more drinks and I had the privilege of smoking one of his Cuban cigars. This was the side of Fred I remembered from his early days. He could be an okay geezer sometimes, but not very often.

'I'm okay, I just want you to know that I think you're a loyal member of the Firm, that's all.'

I just sat there and was wondering what he was on. He wasn't pissed and his mood was better than I'd seen it in a long time.

'Thanks mate that means a lot to me.'

I put my hand out to him. He took it with a firm grip and raised his glass with the other hand and said: 'Here's to Friday.'

I raised mine and simply said. 'Friday.'

Fred told me to help myself to another drink while he went and got my money. I sat there looking at the photos of Fred's family and friends. He had them everywhere and, for a moment, I felt guilty for what I was doing. I had to think back to some of those days when Fred gave me a hard time and, by doing that, it soon brought me back down to earth. I was now back to hating the bastard again. In the meantime Cheryl stuck her head around the door to say hello and asked after Han and Junior.

Raising my hand with the Cuban cigar in it I said to her: 'Is he on drugs or something Cheryl?'

She knew he was tight with his cigars and just laughed and said: 'You are probably in his good books Jack and I think he's wondering who his friends are at the moment.'

I smiled and took another drag on the fat cigar and thought: *'Perhaps I am Cheryl, I just wonder for how long?'*

I could hear Fred making his way back and Cheryl slipped back out of the study, saying goodbye as she disappeared behind the door. Fred came through the door with a leather holdall similar to the one he gave me before, only this one was bigger. He never threw the bag at me this time, but laid it at my feet and said: 'There you go nipper, it's all there including the Yardies'. Are you happy now?'

I never checked the contents in front of Fred because that would be seen as disrespectful. You were expected to accept that the contents were right. I have known some bosses to rip off their blokes by leaving a few grand out of the bag. When they went back to complain they were, in the Firm's eyes, being disrespectful and basically calling the boss a thief. But I had never had that experience with Fred; he was always straight down the line when *my* money was involved.

I smiled and said to him: 'Thanks mate, that will do nicely.'

Having that bag next to me had a wonderful feeling attached to it. Its contents were important because that was going to sustain my family and me for the next few years. I carried on chatting with Fred about Friday night. It was to be quite simple really. Elroy and I were to be at the car park before Fred and Joey turned up. On their arrival they would see Elroy dressed as the Yardie. Fred was to stay in his car and Joey and I were to walk over to Elroy with his money, and it was at that point that I was to whack Joey. What Fred did not know was that instead of me going over to Elroy, I was to return to the car and whack Fred, keeping it nice and simple.

I told Fred that I would call him at nine on Friday to confirm I was in place and all was okay at the park. He would have expected me to do a recon on the place because that would have been the normal format for this type of work. When I drove out of Fred's drive onto the main road, I let out a huge roar to relieve my head of the pressure that had built up. I felt like an actor who had just played the leading role with a bad migraine attack. I took some deep breaths and settled down to the speed limit. The last thing I needed was getting a pull by the Old Bill with a bag full of money next to me. The fact was that I was amazed that I had got this far with the plan. I had never done anything like this before and couldn't afford to take any chances because, quite simply, there were none to be taken. One fuck-up and I would lose my whole family.

I got back home but Han was out with Junior, probably down her mother's making a last farewell. We had told her mum that we were going over to Spain for a few months and she was the only one who knew we were off. I poured myself a large brandy and sat down on the settee and took some 'me time'. I just stayed in silence for twenty minutes to collect my thoughts and control my breathing. This was one of the best things I picked up on my travels to India.

After my quiet time, I counted out the money. It was all there as expected and was all in low denominations which made it so much easier to launder. At that moment, Han walked in with Junior on one arm and a bag of shopping on the other, making her way through to the kitchen. As she came along side of me, she stopped dead in her tracks and said loudly: 'Fuck me! Jack is that all ours?'

I picked up two handfuls of cash and waved it in front of me and excitedly said: 'You see this Han, this is what it's all about, this is our future, this is what we have been working for!'

She hurriedly went upstairs and put Junior in his cot for a nap and came back down. She gave me her sexy look and knew from experience it would cost me money.

'What is babe?'

She was on all fours and came crawling towards me on the sofa like a tiger hunting its prey. She came very close to my face and blew gently in my ear. She knew I loved what she was doing and I felt shivers run up and down my body. She began to talk gently into my ear, real filthy stuff she knew I liked to hear. She was working me big time and I loved every bit of it.

'You love my tits darling don't you?'

I whispered back: 'You know I do baby.'

'Well you know you've always said that you'd like them bigger? Well... I butted in and said: 'If it's a boob job babe you're after, then you got it.'

She went to give me a huge cuddle, but I stopped her and gave her a serious look and said: 'One condition though.'

She stopped right in her tracks and cupped both my cheeks and brought her face right up to mine and said: 'What condition Jack?'

'That I pick the size okay?'

She hummed a bit and squeezed both my cheeks and kissed me on the tip of my nose.'

'Okay darling, you got a deal.'

Then jumped off me and went into the kitchen.

I shouted from the lounge: 'Was that it then, don't I get no more?'

She stuck her head back in the doorway and laughed and said:

'Don't worry Jack. When you get me the tits of your dreams, you won't be able to get enough of them.'

Then she turned and went back into kitchen. I followed her in and asked if she was all sorted for tomorrow.

'Well there isn't much to work out is there? I know why you are getting little Jack christened.'

'Go on then babe, why?'

'Just in case something happens to you; and you want Junior to be Catholic don't you?'

I could have gone on to tell her the real reasons but it was much easier to just leave it at that. I might scare her even more.

I asked her to contact Simone, my accountant, to collect the money in order to get it laundered and stashed.

Hannah told me that Elroy had been on the phone and would I ring him?

It was obvious he had my car and piece ready for me. I left the house and used a pay phone a few streets down. I instructed Elroy to leave the four x four at the car park. There, he would see my car parked up in a bay. I told him to leave the Uzi in the boot of my car where he would find his money for the piece. Then he was told to be at my house by seven thirty on Friday.

After my chat with Elroy I drove my car to the car park and left it in the bay with the boot unlocked. I knew it would be all sorted within a couple of hours so I took a slow walk to my local pub. As I entered the pub, I just managed to see the tail end of Joey disappearing through the crowd. It was then that I got collared by Sammy who was at the bar.

'Jack me old son, how have you been?'

I tried to act as normal as possible, but I wasn't expecting this situation.

Sammy said:' What you having Jack?'

'Get me a brandy mate. Where's Joey gone?'

'He's gone for a piss mate, he won't be long.'

I said to Sammy: 'What are you two doing in here?'

'We just stopped off to wet our whistles, it's thirsty work this crime business.'

I pretended to be amused at his answer, but I knew there was more to this than met the eye. Just then, Joey came up behind me and rested his arm across my shoulders giving the impression that we were best of buddies.

'Hello Jack, what you doing in here mate?'

I said to him: 'I was just putting the same question to Sammy.'
'Just stopping by on a bit of business.'
He then winked at me, as if I was meant to know.

I said fuck all and supped on my drink. Sammy moved away from us to another crowd to mingle, and then Joey leaned over and whispered in my ear.

'Fred's put me in the picture Jack and Sammy knows fuck all if that's the reason for the troubled look on your face bro'. I just wanted to take a look at the place, that's all.'

I knew there and then that he was feeding me a line of bullshit, but I wasn't going to ask too much and just nodded in agreement. My gut feeling had come into play and was telling me to beware. I made small talk with Joey for a while and then made an excuse to leave and said my goodbyes. Once outside the pub, I felt a shiver go right down my spine; like death walking right through me. I was deeply concerned about Joey being there, as well as having Sammy with him. It didn't make sense and, to be honest, Joey had just fucked my day up big time. I took a slow walk around the block and made my way back to the car park. True to form, Elroy had parked up a brand new four-x-four Shogun next to my Jag. I took a quick look about and then went to the boot and inside was my Uzi.

As I left for home, my mind was going ten to the dozen. I parked up in the garage and put some disposable gloves on and went to the boot to retrieve the gun.

I placed it on my work bench and started to take it apart bit by bit to make sure all the parts were not worn out. These fuckers had a tendency to jam if they weren't kept in good order. This weapon was perfect as I examined each component. I was able strip down a firearm blind-folded after being taught by an old gangster I knew when I was a younger.

Han came into the garage to see what was keeping me occupied and her eyes lit up when she saw the gun in pieces on the bench.

'Wow Jack, what's that?'

Before I could answer, she came over and picked up the hand grip.

'Is this the special gun you were talking about?'

I watched her hold and caress the weapon almost as if she was both frightened and titillated by it; it was weird to see.

'Yes it is babe. An Uzi 9mm machine pistol capable of firing a100 rounds in seconds.'

I asked her to make me a cup of tea while I finished cleaning it and putting it back together. She never heard a word I said because she was mesmerised by the gun. Eventually, she said: 'One hundred rounds. Wow Jack, that must do some damage.'

I was getting a bit concerned now and said: 'Look babe, forget about the piece and go and put the kettle on. I'm getting a bit worried about you'

'Guns fascinate me Jack, they always have.'

I said to her: 'I've noticed' and promised her that when we get to India she could have a go on my collection of rifles I had out there. She acted like a big kid by saying: 'Can I Jack? You promise?'

I had begun to notice things like that in her that there might be more to Hannah than I'd realised. I don't think I would like to upset her if there was a gun in the house because she was giving the impression that she wouldn't have too many qualms about using it. I put the Uzi back together, happy with its condition, and passed it to Hannah to look at. Just watching her point the gun and imitating gunshot noises fascinated me. After a little while, I decided playtime was over but Han thought differently and started acting out. I had to grab hold of her and prize the gun out of her hands.

Once I stashed the Uzi away, I went into the kitchen. I was sitting at the table in deep thought while Han was at the sink washing up.

'How did it go with Elroy?'

I stayed silent, just staring at the floor in deep reflection.

She raised her voice to get my attention.

'Jack! Did you hear what I just said?'

I came back to earth a bit sharpish and turned to acknowledge her.

'Yeah babe, it all went like clockwork.'

She started to dry her hands and said: 'Well what is wrong then darling?'

I looked up at her and said:

'I bumped into Joey and Sammy in the King's Head.'

Sounding surprised she said: 'They never use that pub.'

'I know sweetheart; that's what's bothering me.'

I told her about my conversation with Joey.

'So what's wrong then?'

I replied: 'What's wrong Han is that no one is meant to know about this work, apart from the three of us: Fred, me and Joey.'

She asked: 'How did Sammy get involved then?'

'That's what I mean sweetheart. Joey made a point of telling me that Sammy knew nothing about Friday.'

'Oh I see. Do you think Fred is up to something?'

'I don't know; it's been doing my head thinking about it. My gut is telling me that something is wrong, but for the life of me I can't put my finger on it. There's one thing I'm sure of: there is something not right because I can feel it.'

Chapter Thirteen

'Calm before the storm'

I went to bed early that night because we were getting Junior christened the next morning. I was dead tired; it had been a long day and my head was pounding. I tossed and turned and slept restlessly unable to get Fred out of my mind.

My alarm was set for 6 am, but I had been awake since five just cuddling Hannah. I loved listening to her when she was asleep. She would make sweet little sniffle-like sounds and lightly grind her teeth. She would never believe me that she made these noises until I recorded her. Hannah would jokily threaten to do me serious damage whilst I was asleep if I ever told anyone. It was silly little things like this that made me love Hannah. We were always messing around and acting like a couple of kids, so we were not only lovers we were great mates as well.

I got up and went straight into the shower cubicle and stood under the warm revitalising water with my arms stretched out onto the wall looking downwards, my thoughts were still focussed on Sammy. Han burst into the bathroom to use the loo and told me my suit and clothes were ready and laid out for me downstairs.

I brought Junior down to have his breakfast and put him in his highchair. Hannah hurriedly made her way around the kitchen sorting breakfast for us.

'You know Jack, today doesn't feel like Junior's christening, it just feels like any other day.'

I could tell she wasn't happy with the arrangements that had been made. To make her feel better, I told her she could have a proper christening once this business was over and done with. She stopped pouring the tea and said: 'I want the best for our child.'

'You got it. We'll have the works okay babe?'

She smiled and said: 'Okay then Jack we'll treat this christening as only temporary, so no one needs to know about it until we have the proper one.'

I smiled and replied: 'Sounds good to me. So can we just get on with this today without you throwing a wobbler?'

'Of course we can darling. Now I know I can have the type of christening I've always wanted for our boy, I'll be as good as gold.' she said with that cheeky grin of hers.

After breakfast Han was running around sorting Junior out. I remembered that Han had been playing about with the piece the night before so I decided to give it another clean.

Just then the phone rang.

It was Father Malone to ask us if we were still happy to go ahead that morning.

'Of course Father, what made you say that?'

He laughed and said: 'Hannah, that's why Jack.'

I knew what he was talking about because he obviously thought Hannah would have put up an argument with what I had sorted out. I told him that we compromised and now all's sweet.

'Well done Jack, see you soon then.'

Hannah came to me to ask who had been on the phone. I explained what Father Malone had said and how surprised he was that she had gone along with my christening plan.

She asked: 'Did you tell him that we were to have a proper one later Jack?'

I shrugged my shoulders and told her I couldn't because the chances were we would be doing it in India, and I wouldn't want to hurt his feelings.

She came over to me and gave me a cuddle and said: 'You do care about others Jack, don't you?'

I just smiled and said: 'When it comes to a priest darling, there's no point lying, so it's best to just leave the other christening out of it. That way I haven't got to lie to him.'

We left our house for the church. Han sat in the back of the car giving Junior a feed. I would often look at her in the rear view mirror when she had Junior in her arms and I could see that he was the most precious thing on earth to her. She absolutely adored our son and I dearly loved them both which made me a very lucky geezer. We drove into the vestry driveway and parked up. Father Malone came out to greet us dressed in his robes.

'Hannah my child, it is so good to see you, and who do we have here then?'

He pulled back the lace blanket that was wrapped around Junior, exposing his face. Father Malone's eyes lit up when he saw the boy.

'He has his mother's eyes and looks so let us pray he has none of his father's traits.' He looked up at me and winked. I had to laugh at the cheek of the old bugger.

'Let's all go in for a dram to wet Junior's head before we start shall we?'

I was sure that he was an alcoholic because everything that happened around him involved a drink in it. But he was a lovely man and I thought the world of him. He never once judged me, yet he knew everything about me and he knew I wanted to change. I suppose that was why we became close. Once inside, he had his bottle out and was pouring the whiskey into glasses and handed one to Han and me.

'A toast to Jack Junior, may our Lord Jesus be his companion throughout life.'

Han looked at me and smiled as we raised our glasses. Both of us said in unison: 'To Junior, may God bless him.'

We drank the whiskey in one gulp and I could see that Han hated the taste because she pulled a face like a kid having its medicine. We weren't whiskey drinkers. Especially Hannah; she was more of a wine drinker and I was a beer and brandy man.

Father Malone then said: 'Let's get started and get this laddie under the protection of the Holy Spirit.'

We followed him through the hallway leading into the church and up to where the font was positioned. Little Junior was being as good as gold. Even when the Holy water was poured over his dark curly hair, he didn't utter a sound. The service only lasted fifteen minutes, after which we were heading back to his study, to wet Junior's head again, no doubt. Han had said as we followed him back through the hallway that she didn't want to hang about too long because she had a lot to do. I agreed with her because it was near on D-Day and I wanted to make sure all was in order.

'Cheers Father for doing that for us.' I said as I handed him a bundle of notes. Han and I raised our drinks.

He stuffed the notes under his tunic and said: 'It was my pleasure Jack. Now I hope I will see more of the three of you here at the church.'

I never answered and just smiled and made our excuses to leave. As I said before, I didn't want to lie to him. I would tell him all once the work had been completed. After we left, I dropped Han and Junior off at her mum's and I went to a phone box and belled Fred.

'You okay Jack?'

'No, not really Fred. Is it alright to pop around for a cuppa?'

There was a pause then he answered: 'Sure Jack, see you soon.'

I needed to talk with him about the pub meeting with Joey and Sam. This time, as I drove into Fred's driveway, I noticed that the Roller had gone. Fred opened the door and I gestured to the empty space where his roller had been.

'The garage took it away this morning for repairs. Come in and tell me what's up.'

I followed him in to his study shutting the door behind me. Fred went to his chair and dropped into it and took a cigar out of a box on the desk. As he rolled it between his fat fingers and smelling it, he made eye contact with me and said: 'Well?'

Before answering, I looked apprehensively over at Fred to see if I could suss if there was anything wrong. I then said: 'No doubt you've heard that I bumped into Joey and Sammy at the King's Head.'

Fred stayed focussed on me and replied: 'So, what's the problem Jack?'

I fired right back and said: 'Sammy. Sammy's my problem Fred. Why would he be with Joey when he's meant to be looking over the meeting place?'

Fred went through the process of lighting his cigar in silence. During that short time the only sound was coming from him was the puffing on the end of it to get it lit and glowing.

I carried on after the pause: 'What I want to know is why Joey would be looking at the meeting place? It doesn't make sense mate.'

Fred sat up in his chair and said.

'Jack, stop reading too much into it. Did I not tell you to leave Joey to me?'

I replied: 'Yeah you did Fred.'

'Well let me worry about Joey because everything is sorted and under control?'

I went on to tell him that having Sammy so close to home was not a very bright idea. Fred's face changed to a real serious one and said: 'I hope you're referring to Joey with that last comment Jack.'

I felt like blurting out exactly how I felt, but I had to stay in control and not lose my temper, especially at this stage of the game. I lied to keep him sweet.

'Of course I'm talking about Joey.'

'Well, like I say, leave him to me. Now, is everything sorted for tomorrow?'

'It's all in place. Just drive into that car park at ten thirty with the bright spark.'

Fred let out a laugh when I said that.

'Fuck me Jack; you really do hate him don't you? I should've dropped my price on him because I reckon you would've whacked him for fuck all.'

I said nothing and just smiled at him.

'Now Jack, I'm a busy man and I've got a lot on today, so if there's anything else on your mind, then say it now.'

I looked across at Fred and said: 'No that's it mate so I'll see you tomorrow.'

'Tomorrow it is then. See yourself out.'

I walked out of his study not knowing what to think. One bit of me felt I was getting paranoid, but another part of me was warning that something was wrong. The fact was that there was fuck-all I could do about it and would have to carry on with the plan.

When I got home I parked the car outside the house and nipped into the garage and grabbed the gun, which had been wrapped and sealed in an airtight bag. My plan was to hide it in the park so I wouldn't have to carry it with me on the night. As I made my way to the park to stash the piece, the weather was perfect, with heavy rain and thunder. It was ideal for keeping people away. I knew where I was going to stash the Uzi and pulled up as close as possible. I took a quick look around just to be sure no one was about, and then disappeared into the undergrowth where I hid it.

As I left the park, I was extra vigilant, making sure there was no one about or tailing me. This would be the normal thing to do on this type of work. Every job had its own modus operandi and on this one, it was important that I was not seen in the park area. Also, I had to lay low and stay out of sight for the few days leading up to the work.

I went home to sort out my work wear for the following evening. I found Hannah packing a couple of suitcases. Watching her pack was something else. I had to remind her that she was only meant to bring the bare essentials and not the kitchen sink.

I asked her: 'Did you sort the rest of that money out babe?'

'Yes sweetheart, I gave it all, except Elroy's, over to Simone as you wanted.'

Simon was my banker cum accountant, and the only difference between him and the rest of his profession was that he was a dodgy bastard. He dealt with all my cash money and set up my offshore accounts. His speciality was laundering large amounts of money, at which he was an expert in the field. His fees were reasonable and I had always trusted him and kept him out of the clutches of Fred and the Firm. If this piece of work went wrong, I knew my money would be safe with Simon.

I told Hannah of my meeting with Fred.

'Do you still think something isn't right darling?'

I replied: 'Fred isn't giving off any vibes babe. I just can't read him at all, I'm hoping I'm wrong.'

Han tried to reassure me.

'Let's put it this way Jack, everything is going the way you want it to.'

She was right. It was and I replied: 'The plan had been going really well until I bumped into Joey and Sammy.'

'Perhaps you're just getting a bit paranoid, have you thought of that?'

I had to think about what she was saying because she had a point; things were going very well for me and I wasn't really used to that. Perhaps Han was right about me getting paranoid. There was nothing else to go on, so I just put it down to that and got on with the plan.

After we ate that evening, Hannah went upstairs and put Junior down for the night. I went over to our drinks cabinet and poured myself a brandy. Just then, Han came into the room and asked me to pour her the same.

I said: 'It's not like you to want a brandy babe, are you nervous about tomorrow?'

She took the drink from me and looked me in the eyes and said: 'I'm not so much worried about me Jack, but the way you have been acting since you bumped into those two has me worrying for you.'

I smiled and said: 'Does it show that much?'

'Yes it does show, so stop worrying and get your act together. You need to get back on track; otherwise you won't be right for Junior and me.'

I couldn't believe I was hearing these wise words of wisdom coming from a girl half my age. She was streetwise enough to see that things weren't right with me and it was that that was bothering her.

'Han, I have an idea babe that you're going to jump at.'

Those words got her attention and she said: 'What's that then Jack?'

I stood there wondering if I was doing the right thing when I said to her: 'I want to give you a piece for Junior's and your protection, but I'm worried that you might fuck about with it.'

She came over to me all excitedly with that kiddie look all over her face. I held her by both her arms and put my face right up to hers and said: 'Listen to me, this is not a game. You must take this seriously, okay?'

'Do you mean a gun Jack?'

I gripped her arms tighter and said to her: 'Well I didn't mean a fucking spear sweetheart.'

'I'll be okay with that Jack, especially if I've got Junior with me. If anyone came near our kid you know I would fucking shoot the bastards.'

'That's what I'm afraid of Hannah that you end up shooting the wrong person.'

'Look Jack I am not that stupid. If anyone apart from you or Elroy tries to get near us, then I'll shoot them, I promise Jack.'

I smiled at her and said: 'That's all there is to it sweetheart; nice and simple. If anyone opens that car door other than Elroy or me, then just pull the trigger.'

She pulled me close to her and said: 'What gun can I use babe?'

I had decided to let her use my Colt .45 automatic which can hold thirteen bullets, including one in the pipe. All she would have to do is point it at the target and pull the trigger and whatever was in front of her would be blown away.

'You can have the 45 auto babe. Wait here and I'll get it so that you can get the feel of it, okay.'

Eager and compliant, she said: 'Okay love.'

I went into the garage and returned with the piece and two pairs of disposable gloves. I threw a pair at her and told her to put them on. Then I handed her the gun and her face lit up like a neon sign as she started to caress and stroke it. Han's facial expression changed to a look I had seen many times before with trained killers. All hit men loved their weapon of choice and they would caress it and almost treat it as a family member because they had so much respect for it. Now, I was seeing the same look in Hannah. I knew there was more to her than met the eye; I also knew she was quite capable of using it if she had to.

I kept it simple when instructing her on how to use it. It was important that she understood the safety catch mechanism. The good thing with Han was that, she was a quick learner and within half an hour, she was handling the gun like a professional.

'Well, do I get your approval then?'

I answered by saying: 'With flying colours sweetheart. Now you've got the idea, don't end up shooting me, okay?'

'When do I get the shells?'

'Don't worry that beautiful little head of yours about bullets. You can have a full clip when we leave tomorrow.'

'Can I sleep with it Jack?'

I turned towards her and said: 'Fuck me Hannah, now I am getting worried about you again.'

She just laughed and ran upstairs with the gun to put it under her pillow.

Chapter Fourteen

'D-Day'

Next morning I was up at five and was surprised to find that I had slept so long considering it was D-Day. I slid out of the bed leaving Han tangled up in the duvet. She would do that if she'd had a restless night. My guess was she had been worrying about this bit of business. I had to keep remembering that she was a complete novice with this line of work. I went to check on Junior, who was lying flat on his back sleeping contently.

I made my way downstairs to take my 'me time': one of the most important parts of my day. After taking half an hour of self-reflection, I felt good. My mind was now focussed on tonight's work and I was eager to get it over and done with. I felt much happier knowing that Hannah would be tooled up. Even though my gut feeling was still there, it wasn't as bad as it had been.

I made a bottle and some breakfast for Junior and brought him downstairs. He was honking, and having to change him would sometimes turn me a funny shade of green, but I loved it really because he was my son. I sat him opposite watching him pick his food up with his hands and stuffing as much as he could into his mouth. He did make me laugh and feel happy. It was this happy feeling that throughout my life I had never experienced before. Only now it was becoming an everyday occurrence and I loved it. I was not cut out to be a contract killer anymore. I did have a shallow fondness, the respect that came with being a gangland 'player', but respect only lasts as long as your face fits. I'd had enough of it now because Hannah and Junior were now the focus of all my dreams and hopes.

Hannah came downstairs looking like she had been dragged through a hedge backwards and just sat at the table not saying a word. I had learnt from experience that it was never a good idea to talk to her when she was like this. I just gave her a coffee and left her to it. After a few minutes and a few gulps of coffee, she responded to Junior who was calling out for her. She went over and picked him up and gave him a cuddle. She looked around the kitchen and noticed that I had fed and changed him.

Hannah smiled and said: 'Thanks babe.'

'What for darling?'

She came over to me with Junior still in her arms and cuddled up to me and said: 'For putting up with me when I was ill and for being a great dad to our boy.'

I felt well chuffed that she appreciated that I had kept my promise and helped her through her illness. Before she became ill, she wouldn't let me lift a finger around the house because she got it into her head that she was there to look after me, which she did. But after her operation it was agreed that I would help as much as possible; and the thing was I enjoyed it. I was now learning to be a father; something I never had a chance to do with my other kids.

Affectionately I said: 'Thanks sweetheart, it's nice to be nice.'

She looked up at me and kissed me on the lips and then Junior wanted his share of loving as well and leaned forward between us with his wet mouth wide open and gave us both sloppy wet kisses. We stood there laughing and enjoying our child just like a normal couple would. I knew then that this is what I was fighting for.

Hannah went on to say that she had been restless all night and hadn't slept well because she had been having nightmares. Also, it didn't help with her having her period.

'Are you all ready for tonight Jack?'

I poured her another coffee and said I had everything in place and just wanted to get it out of the way.

She said: 'It won't be long now.'

She was right, it wouldn't be that long now and by this time tomorrow, it would be all over. After breakfast was out of the way, I took the car down to the carwash and had a valet job done on it. Just as a precaution, I wanted to make sure that my car was nice and cleansed of any forensic. It didn't really need it, but I was just playing safe. After all, Elroy had been in the car when he left the Uzi and, for all I knew, he could have sneezed or coughed, leaving some form of residue behind.

I was going to use my own car as the second vehicle for tonight's work, leaving it well out of the way of the car park. I was to be tucked up in the undergrowth out of sight until Fred and Joey turned up. The plan for the evening was easy really and the only thing that could fuck it up was if a load of people turned up. But my timing for that night was perfect for that park. It was usually dead quiet at that time and the cars left in the parking bays belonged to the local residents, so I was happy with the set-up.

I was thinking about contacting my kids from my previous marriage just in case something went wrong with this bit of work. We hadn't been in touch for a long time now. They had disowned me when they realised that their father was a villain and that it was he who instigated the divorce from their mother. However, I had enough to do and very little time to do it in. So I thought I would leave that idea alone for another day. Once I got the car back, it was spotless. I did love it and would sometimes near on have a climax when polishing it. Hannah would call it an extension of my dick or accuse me of spending more time rubbing the car than I did her, but that's the effect a Jaguar had on me.

It was late afternoon before I got back home. I had decided to take a drive out into the country to help me think and relax. As soon as I got through the front door, I nearly tripped ass over tit because Hannah had the bags packed and ready by the door. Our plan was for me to drive up to the Shogun at 9:30 with Han and Junior, get Elroy to put the cases in the back compartment leaving Han and Junior in the rear seat. That left me an hour to park my car up and get my piece out from the undergrowth and plot up to wait for Fred and Joey.

Elroy was to show himself by getting out of the Shogun when Fred dipped his lights. Then Joey and I were to go over to pay him and get the info. It was then that I was to whack Joey in front of our Yardie man Elroy. That was the plan that Fred thought was going to happen, but unbeknownst to him, it was to be very different.

I angrily called out to Hannah: 'Hannah!'

She started to come down the stairs realising from the tone of my voice that I was not a happy bunny. She had stopped halfway down the stairs and said: 'Yes Jack, what's wrong sweetheart?'

I looked down at the suitcases and just pointed my forefinger at them and then turned to look at her.

'What's up? I've only packed two cases and the other bag has Elroy's money, our flight documentation and passports in it.'

I angrily said to her: 'It's not how many bags you've bloody packed or what's in them that's the problem. What's pissed me off is that you have left them right by the front door. Didn't you realise, I could've come through that door with Fred and if that was the case, what the fuck would I say to him: *'By the way Fred, Han and me were just nipping off for a well-*

earned break after I've just whacked your son in law!'

Han rushed down the rest of the stairs as I marched into the kitchen. She tried to carry the bags into the garage while I just sat at the kitchen table fuming. She was doing her best not to struggle with the bags but banged into everything as she came through the kitchen. She went back for the second bag and dropped it on the kitchen floor, then turned to me and said: 'Look Jack, I am sorry for the balls-up with the cases, but I'm not a professional like you and I don't think like you either. I just want you to know that I never meant to do wrong, honest!'

Then she burst into tears and I now felt like a right asshole for popping her out. I got up and went over to her and gave her a cuddle.

'I'm so sorry for having a go at you; it's just that I'm stressed as fuck. I was okay until the bag incident and it was that, that set me off. I really am sorry babe. Now wipe your eyes and go make a cup of tea while I put these away.'

'Thanks Jack. I am sorry for being stupid sometimes.'

'You're not stupid Han, far from it babe. You were right when you said that you don't think the same as me. It's me that should be saying sorry to you.'

'I love you Jack.'

I turned to her and saw her lovely little face with tears running down her cheeks and I replied: 'I love you more Hannah'

We both smiled at each other because that was our running joke between us: who loved each other the most.

We sat down to eat and there wasn't much conversation coming from either of us. We were both in deep thought and the only sounds were coming from Junior as he slurped his juice with a straw. We both laughed at him making those noises which broke the silence and soon we were talking about the plan.

We were all ready now and Elroy was due to be belling within the next few minutes. I had got Hannah's gun and put the ammunition into it and carefully put it in a sack bag. Hannah had been told not to touch the gun without her gloves on. Just then the phone rang. Han and I momentarily looked at each other and without a word being said, we knew it was time. I got up to answer the phone.

'Hello.'

'It's me Jack, parked up and sorted.'

I replied: 'Be with you shortly mate.'

I then turned to Hannah and said: 'Right sweetheart we're in business. We're giving it an hour and I'll run you up to Elroy. In the meantime, put on those clothes you picked out and put Elroy's money in your bag. Don't forget to put the gloves on.'

I reminded her that her gloves were not to come off under any circumstances. She went off to sort herself out and I put the cases in the boot of the Jag. I went over to the workbench and got the piece and took it out of its sack and placed it in the car. Han had previously checked the flight times from Gatwick, so we had a timetable of the available flights. We were now ready to go.

I called out to Han who came down the stairs with Junior. I told her to get in the back of the jag and settle Junior down. I went around the house and left certain lights on as well as the TV to give the impression we were at home. I made a mental checklist and was satisfied all was in order. Then I belled Fred to let him know all was okay. This was crunch time now and I was buzzing with adrenalin; it was a better buzz than a line of top quality Cocaine. We took a steady drive towards the park, avoiding the main streets and sticking to the side roads just to avoid anyone noticing us. Han and I were in deep thought and never spoke during the short trip. Junior was sound asleep in Hannah's arms.

As I pulled in to the park, it was dimly lit, the only light coming from the few lamp posts that were dotted around the surrounding area. We headed to where Elroy was parked up and pulled alongside. I got out of my car and opened the boot and transferred the cases to the back of the Shogun.

Hannah and Junior climbed into the rear seat where I handed her the gun, reminding her that the safety catch was on. She put Junior next to her with a blanket wrapped around him to keep him warm. Then quite calmly, she put the .45 under her coat, resting it on her knee. I leaned forward to kiss her and to reassure her that everything would be alright and that Elroy was there to protect her, as well as me. I also reminded her that if she had to use the gun then she was to make sure she shot the right people. She gave out a little false laugh and told me to piss off, but to be careful. As I went to pull away from her, she grabbed me by the lapels and pulled me back to her and kissed me passionately.

'You make sure you come back to us Jack because we both love and want you in our lives. So don't fuck up.'

I wasn't sure if I was getting a compliment or a bollocking.

I shut the door and went to the front where Elroy was seated. Through the window I said to him: 'You ready mate?'

'I'm cool Jack. Has Han got my money?'

'Yes she has mate and you'd better make sure you earn it, okay?'

'I will Jack, you can rely on me.'

I looked at him and held my hand out. We both shook hands and I said to him: 'I know I can Elroy, now make sure you turn that interior light off before opening the door because you will be lit up like a Christmas tree?'

'Fuck me Jack, I forgot about that.'

'Well it's a good job I didn't.'

I got back into my Jag where I glanced over my shoulder to see if I could get a final glimpse of Hannah before I drove off. But she had put herself out of sight in the rear of the Shogun. I drove away slowly out of the car park to tuck my car up in a safe area just outside. We had about forty-five minutes to go before Fred and Joey were due to turn up. With a job like this, it was important to arrive on time to do the business and get away as quick as possible. Fred would have known that I would check the surrounding area, making sure it was all clear. It was impossible to check the whole area because the park was too large.

I made my way into the undergrowth, retrieved the Uzi and took it out from its sealed bag. I was wearing a three-quarter length leather coat which had the pocket lining removed. The purpose for that was to conceal and handle my piece without taking the coat off. I also wore a '40s' style hat. It resembled an American gangster hat and kept my face in the shade. I moved to a spot where I could get a clear view of the park entrance.

Dead on 10:30, a pair of headlights came into view from the direction of the park entrance. If our Fred and Joey were on time, then this would be them. I stuck my head out from the bushes and got a good look at the car and saw that it was indeed them. I had both hands in my pockets gripping the gun firmly under my coat. I had three-quarters of the jacket buttons undone and walked up to their car from behind. I made my way around to the driver's door and tapped on the window. The sound of the electric window was quite loud as it wound down when I was face to face with Fred and Joey.

Fred said: 'Is he here Jack?'

'He's over the other side of the parking lot Fred.'

Fred then asked: 'Have you got his money?'

'Yes.'

I patted my chest to give him the impression it was under my coat,

'Now flash your lights Fred.'

Fred did as he was told and immediately, a pair of lights flashed back from the opposite end of the parking lot.

Fred turned to Joey and roughly said: 'Right you. Out you get and go with Jack.'

Joey never said a word and just got out of the car and came round to my side of the car. I asked Fred to flash his lights again and, once he did, we all saw the outline of Elroy's frame get out of the Shogun and stand next to it.

This was my cue and I said to Joey: 'After you mate.'

Joey gave me a patronising smirk and stepped in front of me. He now had his back to me as I turned to Fred and gave him a knowing wink. I raised my right arm up from under my coat exposing the Uzi. I then brought my left hand around and held the short nozzle to steady it.

It was then I opened fire and all I could see were the flashes as each round discharged from the gun. As each bullet hit his body the force sent Joey flying through the air like a rag doll. There was no aim with this weapon; it just hit everything in front of it. Joey ended up about fifteen yards away face down in the muddy ground. I walked over to his lifeless body to inspect the damage. I could see from the dim light that half his head was missing exposing pieces of his brain, the rest of which had been scattered around his body. The whole of his back was a mass of blood-stained holes and from the look of him, I don't think one shell missed its mark.

I heard Fred get out of his car and started walking towards me shouting at me.

'What the fuck are you doing you dopey cunt! You're meant to whack him after you've got the info.'

I turned around and raised the smoking gun up and levelled it at him. He stopped in his tracks and his tirade of abuse towards me ceased just as abruptly. Recovering, he said: 'Point that fucking thing away from me Jack and go get the info you stupid cunt.'

I felt the anger of years rise within me and started to walk slowly towards Fred, still pointing the gun at him. He could now see that I was not amused and as I took each step towards him, he took a step backwards. I never said a word as I continued to get closer to him. His face was now showing fear and mine was full of contempt. Fred then said: 'What the fuck are you playing at Jack?'

I kept the gun on him and continued to slowly move towards him.

Again he said: 'What the fuck are you doing?'

I answered him in the way I'd always wanted to and said: 'All's I asked from you was to retire Fred, but instead of letting me go you disrespected me and had me doing your fucking dirty work.'

Fred could see I meant business and began to plead with me.

'Look Jack, you can retire mate and I'll even give you a £500,000 pay off.'

I remained silent and was now only a few metres from him when he did something I never would have thought possible from the likes of him: he first pleaded and then began to beg.

'Please Jack, please don't do this, I'll give you my word that there won't be any comebacks. Haven't I always treated you like family… please Jack, for God sake don't do this… think of Cheryl and my kids.'

'With pent up anger mixed with a perverse pleasure I growled: 'Think of your kids you fucking maggot. You never once considered my Junior when Hannah was ill did you?'

'Please Jack; please Jack, for fuck sake please!'

Listening to him beg and plead for his life only fuelled my anger towards him. I said my last words to him.

'Who's the dopey cunt now Fred?'

'But Jack…'

I opened fire on him with the Uzi. The noise and flashes from the gun were blinding and deafening. I could hear Fred's screams as the first few rounds hit him. I walked towards him keeping my finger on the trigger until the gun ran out of ammo. I stopped and looked down at his lifeless body and took in the surrounding silence. Fred was lying on his back and his face had a fixed look of terror on it with bulging eyes and his mouth wide open. His chest and lower body were full of holes where the bullets had entered him.

It was then that the sounds of gunfire come from Elroy's direction. I heard two distinctive shotgun blasts and my thoughts were instantly on Hannah and Junior. I started to run as fast as I could to where the Shogun was parked. When I got within twenty metres, I heard Hannah scream; then there were at least half a dozen pistol shots.

I ran as quickly as I could to the car and nearly tripped over Elroy. I briefly looked down at him spread-eagled on the ground and saw that his face was completely missing where it had been shot off with what must have been a shotgun. I jumped over his body and saw Hannah come out from behind the Shogun with the .45 in her hand which was still smoking.

I looked into the back and saw Junior still under his blanket I opened the door and put my hand on him to make sure he was okay. He moved as soon as I touched him and the relief was indescribable. I then went up to Hannah and took the piece out of her hand. She was shaking and couldn't talk coherently without bursting in to tears.

I held Hannah in my arms and asked: 'Han who did this to Elroy; what happened?'

She pointed to the other side of the Shogun which was the blind side for me. I levelled Han's gun and grabbed her and pulled her down onto the gravel, not knowing who or what was on the other side of the vehicle. I lay on the ground and looked right under the car. What I saw didn't surprise me because my gut feeling had been right all along. There, lying face up was Sammy with a shotgun at his side. I stood up and made my way around to have a closer look. I could see he was well and truly dead because he had been shot several times in the head and chest.

'Is he dead Jack?'

I looked down at Sammy and then looked back at Han and said: 'He's dead sweetheart, there's no doubt about that.'

I had to think fast and put the Uzi in Elroy's hand and left the .45 on the deck between Elroy and Sammy. I was angry now because it was obvious that our Fred did have something up his sleeve after all.

I had to shout at Hannah to get her to snap out of her shocked state of mind and get her into the Shogun. I helped her into the car where she grabbed Junior and started to cry. I turned the ignition and steered around Elroy's lifeless body.

Hannah said: 'What about Elroy Jack?'

I said to her: 'It's too late for him darling, he's dead.'

'Oh Jack what have I done'

I said to her: 'Han, you just saved Junior's life and your own, you're a fucking gem sweetheart, well done!'

I drove to where our Jag was parked up quickly transferred our suitcases into it. I took hold of Junior and let Hannah get out of the Shogun and handed him back to her as soon as she was in the back of the Jag. She was in shock now and I needed to get us all back home quickly before the bodies were found. I drove home very carefully and parked up in my garage. I got out and opened the back door to where Han was still sitting and told her to get a grip of herself. Bless her as she handed Junior to me she said: 'I'll be okay now.'

I looked at her and smiled and said: 'I'm so fucking proud of you babe, if it wasn't for that gun, then the pair of you wouldn't be here. You used it like a pro would. Thank you for saving my son.'

She said something quite remarkable: 'No Jack, thank you for that gut feeling of yours because if it was not for that and you being as shrewd as you are, then none of us would be here.'

My gut feeling has always been a big part of my life and has saved my ass many times in the past. I never ignore it and hearing Han thank me for it made me feel lucky to possess this instinct. But now it was back to business.

'Right babe I want you to get all that kit off and put it all in a bin liner. Then unpack the suitcases and put the clothes back okay?'

She was back to normal now and stripped right off and put everything in a bin liner as I did. We put some casuals on and I put the bin liner in our small furnace and destroyed the contents. Han put Junior down and came back downstairs. I had cracked open a bottle of brandy and poured us both a drink. We stood either side of the table with the drinks in our hand and looked at each other. I now had a different kind of respect for her. It wasn't just a loving relationship; it was also now a working partnership.

I raised my glass and said: 'Here's to us babe, we fucking done it!'

I gulped it down in one and Han did the same and then asked for another. We both sat there for an hour or so drinking and talking about the night and what went on. I could see that Hannah had got a buzz from blowing Sammy away because she couldn't stop talking about how it felt. I knew there was more to her than just plain *Hannah*, she now had respect but unfortunately, no one was to hear of it.

We didn't sleep much that night and spent most of it talking over what we were to do next. I like things nice and simple and try not to complicate matters too much because when anything gets complicated, trouble inevitably comes looming in from all angles. Han said:

'What shall we do when the Firm finds out about Fred and Joey?'

I looked at her and told her straight: 'Nothing, just act like the other women on the Firm and say fuck all. Just get on with your day as normal. Anyway sweetheart, no one from the Firm will ask you anything about Fred and Joey.'

She said: 'What about you Jack?'

I smiled and said: 'Han this is part of my job. I'm used to fronting this type of thing and remember babe, I have a lot of respect and no one is going to point a finger at me without having good evidence. Just get on with being a mum to Junior and take him out to your mum's. Today is going to be a busy day for me and I won't be around much.'

It was seven in the morning when my mobile rang.

'Hello, Jack?'

'Hello Benny, what gets you on the phone at this time?'

'Have you not heard?'

I had to put on my best performance now and answered: 'Heard what mate?'

'We'll have to meet because it's fucking urgent, you understand?'

'I understand Benny. Meet me at the car lot at the rear office in an hour, okay?'

'Okay Jack, I'll see you there.'

Han came downstairs with Junior and said: 'Is that the start of it Jack?'

I looked up at her as she stood on the stairs and replied: 'Sure is babe and I'm going to play it my way with this lot. Now don't worry yourself and get out and about babe. If you come across any of the wives, just act ignorant, okay?' Our alibi is each other. We stayed in all night with our son; as simple as that, no more, no less.

She smiled and told me she would do her best. I had to grin when she said that because she could sell sand to the Arabs given the chance and I had no worries with her at all.

I had a quick shower and made my way to the car lot. Benny turned up at the same time.

'Morning Jack.'

As we got inside I said to Benny: 'Now what's all this about?'

'It's gone fucking mental.'

'What's gone mental?'

He paused before saying: 'Fred, Joey and Sammy were all whacked last night at Ladywell Park.'

I looked at Benny with a dead straight face, turned and went and sat down behind the office desk and then said: 'Who's responsible Benny?'

'The fucking Yardies Jack. Fred must have had something going down with them. Did you know what Fred was up to?'

'Me, why should I know what Fred is up to, I'm fucking retired, remember?'

He came over to the desk and rested both hands on the top of it and assumed I was going to drop everything and help out.

'Well Jack, it looks like you will have to come out of retirement because we got no one to run the Firm now, what with those three gone.'

I leaned forward and said in a calm and collected voice: 'Listen to me

Benny, I'm retired and I mean what I say. It means I no longer work for the Firm. I'm not coming out of retirement because I am not interested anymore.'

Benny's face dropped like a kid who had just missed Santa Claus.

'Well what's going to happen then?'

I stood upright very fast pushing the chair back against the wall in the process.

'I don't give a flying fuck Benny! I warned Fred loads of times about Joey, but did he listen? Did he fuck! The rest of the Firm warned him as well, did he listen? Did he fuck! What's happened here sounds like revenge to me. Fred never got over getting ripped off and refused to have the patience to deal with the Yardies. I've warned him that they are not to be messed with for fucks sake. But no, Fred knew better didn't he?'

Now I was walking around the office kicking the odd waste bin and filing cabinet, raising my voice a tad to give Benny the right impression.

Benny asked me to calm down because I was making him nervous. I turned to him and said: 'I'll calm down when you assholes accept that I'm out of the game and stop coming to me for the answers because I haven't got any. This Firm is finished mate and in a few weeks, you lot will be working for the other mobs. As soon as this gets out, they'll be gathering like fucking vultures to pick off the Firm's assets. So get it through your nut. It's all over mate. Now I'm going home'

Benny just shrugged his shoulders and said: 'Are you going to pay your respects to the other halves?'

He was referring to Cheryl and Lynne and Sammy's partner.

I answered without compassion in my voice.

'What respect?' Softening, I then added: 'Look Benny, the last thing I need to be doing is going in and out of houses with the Old Bill on the lookout and reporters everywhere. If you have any sense, you'll do the same mate.'

I opened the door to the office and turned back to Benny: 'Put the word out mate about me and let them all know I want fuck all to do with it I'm laying low, okay?'

Benny just nodded his head in agreement as I left.

I got back to my car and went over the way I dealt with the meeting. I smiled to myself because they were all thinking it was the Yardies, and that was exactly what I had planned. Now I knew I would get a visit from the boys in blue pretty soon because I had been around the Firm for years, and they didn't know I was retired. So it would be the normal rounds for them and, provided my alibi stood up, then we had nothing to worry about. As I pulled into my driveway, there was an unmarked police car sitting parked up. I pulled right up close to them and got out of the car. All the doors of the police car opened simultaneously and four plain clothed Old Bill got out. I recognised the DCI because we had crossed paths a few times over the years but he had never got me on anything.

The DCI said; 'Morning Jack.'

I never answered and walked towards my front door with them following behind me. I opened the door and invited them in and went into the lounge and sat down in my armchair.

'What can I do for you gentlemen?' I asked.

The DCI asked me on my whereabouts last night between 9 and 6 that morning.

'I was here all night with Hannah and my son.'

He said to me. 'Is she in?'

I looked around the room and said: 'Well it doesn't look like it does it?'

This lot knew they were wasting their time with me and just went through the motions. They were probably delighted to hear the good news about Fred and Joey's demise. But they had a job to do and that meant asking questions. They went right through the card with me, even asking me if I was now to become the new boss. I only answered the relevant questions and ignored the rest because they were designed to wind me up. I had been about too long in this business and knew all their tricks. They knew it themselves, but give them credit where it's due, they still tried. Just then Han came through the door with Junior and she was immediately taken into the kitchen by two of them. Han was also familiar with the routine and knew what to say, especially about my alibi. They wouldn't be looking at her as a suspect because as traditional villains, we never involved our other halves in our business.

I could smell Junior and it was bad enough to bring on a severe bout of nausea. The two that were in with Hannah came through to the lounge and said to me:

'What are you feeding that boy on, chicken vindaloo and warm Guinness?'

They all laughed at their own joke, but I just sat there and looked at my watch and said with a straight face: 'Is that it then gentlemen? Because I've got a busy day and need to get on.'

They asked me if I would mind if they took a look around the house. I gave them the impression that I didn't mind at all.

'By all means gentlemen, you lot take your time.'

They looked at each other and the DCI said: 'We'll leave it for now Jack but we may be back in touch, okay?'

Even with the Old Bill it was a game of face off. They knew my house would be clean and that they were wasting their time because everything about these murders pointed to gangland rivalry. They also knew how the Firms work. Firms always say nothing to the police and deal with problems themselves. The Old Bill didn't give a toss about the murders of those four in the park. They were more interested in who was to take over and I couldn't help them with that question. After they left, I went and opened the windows because Junior had just cleared the house and I nearly wanted to puke.

Han came in and said: 'It worked then?'

'What worked babe?'

She raised a plastic bag up with the remnants of Junior's last meal. I had to laugh at her and said: 'It certainly did sweetheart.'

Then we both burst out laughing and cuddled, saying how much we loved each other. I knew then that Han had been worth waiting for. Even though there was an age gap between us, it didn't show because we just got on so well together and enjoyed the same things. Now Han had her first taste of blood and was dealing with it like a pro and that just enhanced my love and respect for her.

We had decided to hang around until the funerals and press were out of the way before we left for Goa. We had got this far and a few more weeks of waiting to make it look good wouldn't hurt, would it?

Chapter Fifteen

'Clean Slate'

In the days following the murders, Tommy's body had been found and he was immediately linked to the 'Murders in the Park' that the tabloids were now having a feeding frenzy over.

My message to Benny regarding leaving me out of everything seemed to have got through. My phone had gone silent and no one appeared at my door as I laid low and out of the way. It was just the three of us now and we really loved each other's company. Each day we would go out for long drives in the country and down to the coast. My idea behind doing that was: *'out of sight out of mind.'* Let the rest of the Firm get on with it. If I was not about and being seen to take control of the Firm, then the other mobs, who all wanted a piece, would not consider me as a threat, especially now the word would be out and about that I was retired. So we stuck to our game plan and just acted like a normal family doing ordinary family things and we loved it. This was what I'd always wanted: a clean slate and a new life, but I never realised it during years I spent with the Firm. It had always been Fred & Co first and my family second. Only now I was realising what I had missed out on with my other kids and now understood why they disliked me so much. I couldn't blame them for the way they were with me, nor could I blame my ex-wife for turning them against me. So much was becoming clearer now and my thinking was changing for the better.

I popped in on Father Malone. It had been two weeks since the murders and the heat around them was cooling off. I was very nervous about seeing him because I was about to confess all. As I knocked on his door, Father Malone came up to me from behind. I noticed he had his gardening overalls on with a tool belt around his waist. I had to smile because I could see the top end of a whiskey bottle sticking out.

'Hello Father.'

He looked up at me as he climbed the few steps and replied: 'Hello Jack, I had a feeling I would be seeing you. How are you my son?'

I wasn't going to give him small talk and say all was 'okay' and 'well' because he knew why I was there.

‘I think we need to talk Father.’

He gave me his knowing look and said: ‘Then you’d best come in and wait in my study while I get changed.’

I went into the study, leaving the door ajar and sat down in an armchair. I could hear him outside changing followed by the sound of a bottle being uncorked. I had often wondered how straight geezers like him, even if he *was* a priest, could sit and hear people’s confessions everyday without it having an effect on them. That’s probably how he dealt with it: *Jamieson’s* He came into the study and went straight to the drinks cabinet, opened it and took hold of two glasses. He came and sat opposite me putting them on the table along with the bottle.

I said to him: ‘Getting prepared are we Father?’

He looked at me then asked me if I was okay.

I said: ‘I don’t know Father, if I’m honest.’

‘Do you want confession Jack?’

‘Yeah Father I do, and can you pour me one of those?’ I replied as I pointed at the bottle. He poured two large whiskeys and handed me one. I took a gulp and said: ‘Can we do it now Father because I want this off my plate.’

He smiled at me and replied: ‘Of course we can Jack.’

He put himself side on to me and bowed his head and started with a prayer. I was sitting nervously on the edge of the armchair with my forearms resting on my thighs looking at the floor. I began by telling him that I never had a choice and, as I told him what I had done, he kept blessing me and making the sign of the cross. I told him everything, except about Hannah shooting Sammy.

We went through the routine of my penance and then we both sat there in silence still having no eye contact with each other.

He positioned himself back to where he was before and said: ‘I do not condone what you have done Jack, but I want you to know that I do understand.’

I thanked him and finished my drink and I told him I wanted to leave to be with Hannah. He showed me to the door where he gave me a hug and said: ‘Well done Jack.’

As I stepped outside, he asked me a question.

‘Why did you not mention Sammy, Jack?’

I smiled as I looked at him and replied:

‘Because there’s nothing to mention, that’s why Father.’